Because
of You

Because of You

Lisa Walker

VIKING

VIKING
Published by the Penguin Group
Viking Penguin, a division of Penguin Books USA Inc.,
375 Hudson Street, New York, New York 10014, U.S.A.
Penguin Books Ltd, 27 Wrights Lane,
London W8 5TZ, England
Penguin Books Australia Ltd, Ringwood, Victoria, Australia
Penguin Books Canada Ltd, 2801 John Street,
Markham, Ontario, Canada L3R 1B4
Penguin Books (N.Z.) Ltd, 182–190 Wairau Road,
Auckland 10, New Zealand

Penguin Books Ltd, Registered Offices:
Harmondsworth, Middlesex, England

First published in 1991 by Viking Penguin,
a division of Penguin Books USA Inc.

1 3 5 7 9 10 8 6 4 2

PUBLISHER'S NOTE
This is a work of fiction. Names, characters, places, and
incidents either are the product of the author's imagination or
are used fictitiously, and any resemblance to actual persons,
living or dead, events, or locales is entirely coincidental.

LIBRARY OF CONGRESS CATALOGING IN PUBLICATION DATA
Walker, Lisa.
Because of you/Lisa Walker.
p. cm.
ISBN 0-670-83225-1
I. Title.
PS3573.A425346B44   1991
813'.54—dc20   90-50761

Printed in the United States of America
Set in Bembo
Designed by Jessica Shatan

For my nephew, Zeb

Because
of You

I COULDN'T EVEN BEGIN to say who my first actual boyfriend was, there were so many. Counting the ones I can count I would say I've probably had fifteen or twenty serious boyfriends, of which nine or ten were ones I thought I'd be spending the rest of my life with. If I counted all the others, if I even could, I'd have to give a number and that number would misrepresent the kind of person I really am. All my boyfriends, serious boyfriends and the others, were exclusive events. I believe in monogamy. This doesn't include flings or chance encounters. Those are more like the bike wrecks you have when you're a kid—before you've really mastered how to balance in tricky situations. The first couple of ones are scary. Then you go through the phase where the scrapes are a badge of courage. Then, as you become more skilled, you quit having wrecks at all. The rare ones you do have are such flukes they just become an oddity.

I happen to fall in love very easy. I've been this way since I was a little kid and it was one of the first things my parents found out about me that caused them great disappointment. For my mother this disappointment was more profound, since she didn't believe in the value of men too much. When I would tell her about a boy I thought was cute I could watch her face envision my whole future—one filled with misery and early pregnancies.

I had quite a few guys ask me to marry them when I was young. My first proposal was from Billy Theodore. Billy asked me to marry him and move to New Mexico, where he was going to work on his uncle's oil rigs.

Billy used to come over every night I was home and hang out on my front porch. He was eighteen and bigger physically than most other guys around. He had long hair, a baby face and bad skin. Billy was really cute but I thought he was too dumb. I was the one who did the talking when we were together and it was just to keep there from being so many long, dead silences. But he really did love me, no matter what I did or said or looked like, and I liked him for that. When he asked me to marry him I said, "I can't, I'm only fourteen," and he said, "That's OK. I'll be making six hundred dollars a week on my uncle's rigs."

That's the way Billy talked, one thing never had anything to do with the other.

Even at fourteen the idea of being married to Billy was spooky. I imagined our house would be tiny and dark. Billy would come in from work with stiff, greasy clothes and sit on our junky secondhand furniture that was permanently stained from his clothes and there would just be a lot of canned meals and bright overhead lights and long silences between us. Plus I figured Billy had a high gross-out quotient, which meant he would have definitely turned into a burper and probably a sloppy beer drinker.

But sometimes, when I was older and wondering if I would ever find the perfect guy, I would fantasize Billy differently. I would think that he had gone and gotten real rich and sophisticated from oil money. That instead of being dumb he was subdued and intense and too poetic, romantic and intelligent for earth communication. I would picture Billy coming back to find me and drive me away with him in a pure white, vintage Lincoln Continental.

I had a great-aunt and great-uncle who had married each other when they were fourteen. They lived to be really old. My great-aunt died of cancer caused by eating too many organ meats. One week after she died my great-uncle died. He hadn't been sick, he was just broken-hearted. My whole life I had always heard him say about my great-aunt, "I love this little girl. She looks exactly the same now as the day I married her."

My great-aunt looked really old. Her hair was so thin you could see her scalp and she had long hairs growing out of a big, warty-looking mole on her jaw. But Uncle Chester loved her and I don't believe he ever even knew her mole was there. He had loved and taken care of her a whole lifetime, and in his eyes she would always still be a fourteen-year-old girl.

I guess I believed that was the thing about love. For as long as you were in love it froze time at that moment you first fell in love. It froze time at that place forever.

I ALWAYS KNEW that things had happened fast for my parents. They met, they got married, I was born. My mom had told me it was because of work that when I was born her and my dad lived in separate towns, so I was sent to live with my mom's parents until they figured out where and how they were going to live. It took them five years to figure this out. My sister Angie was born a year after I was and ended up living with my mom because my mom said she felt too guilty to saddle my grandparents with another kid to look after.

I was happy living with my grandparents but whenever my parents would come to see me I'd beg them to take me back with them. My mom would kiss me and whisper in my ear, "Next time."

My grandparents lived in a really small town that was mostly a stretch of highway. No one knew they were passing through Thelma unless they were from the area.

The town of Thelma was a lot like my mom. It looked gentle and pretty but there was a wicked wedge running deep through it. In my mom the wedge was her dissatisfaction, in Thelma it was the highway.

My grandparents' house faced the highway. It was stuccoed white in cake-swirl designs. Green metal lawn rockers sat on the big front porch, which was shaded by fifty-year-old catalpa trees. Inside, even in summer the house felt cool and damp and smelled like cedar and sassafras.

I slept in the same room that had been my mom's when she was a kid. My bed was cornered between two big windows. The window at the foot of my bed faced the garage, a half-circle gravel drive, and an old barn. The side window looked out to the highway. I would lay in my bed at night and stare through the windows at my grandmother's flower gardens or watch the wild kittens that lived and played around the barn. My mom had told me that when she was a little girl she had caught and tamed some of the kittens. She said one of her games with them was to make them go to bed. She'd shove them under a heavy washtub and leave them until they fell asleep. One day she was trying to slide a kitten underneath and the tub fell from her hands on the kitten's neck and broke it. She'd say she never got over that.

A waist-high wooden shed that I was always warned to stay away from was built on my grandparents' back porch. It had a heavy tin shingle cover that you lifted. Tied inside the rim of the shed was a green wooden pail hooked to a fifteen-foot-long chain. I loved to watch my grandparents lower down the pail to get water. They would do it slowly and gently until the chain didn't pull. Then they would let the pail tilt and water would flow into the bucket until its weight had pulled the pail under and swallowed it out of sight. My grandparents never allowed the bucket to hit the water, or let it make a splash.

As soon as the cover to the well was opened an earth smell penetrated the porch and coolness rose up from the water. My grandparents told me to never drop coins or toys or trash into the water and even though I wanted to see how far things would drop or watch the water wave in circles out from the fallen object, I never did.

I spent hours staring down the deep tunnel into the well, watching the dark, calm, colorless surface of the water, which seemed to be there just to hold the cool air above. The tunnel of air was so still that even the quiet echoed to somewhere.

To me the well seemed like all the things in the world I didn't know about. I could see the water but I didn't know where it came from. I didn't know how far or deep or wide it was. I didn't know what was under or around it. It was like someone talking about the atmosphere or the ocean floor, other planets or China. It was like the preacher telling us about being born or dying or heaven or hell. To me the well was what forever was.

A kitten and three chickens had drowned in the well

before when the lid had been left up. This upset my grandparents because the water would be contaminated. I tried to believe that if I looked hard enough into the well I would be able to find the dead animals alive and swimming happily in their new underwater world.

My grandparents were devout Southern Baptists. They believed it was a sin to worship any other belief, idol or savior other than the Baptist version of Jesus Christ. They took me to church every Sunday and on holidays. They read the Bible before bed, they watched Billy Graham on TV, and they talked about God a lot. But really my grandparents worshiped the well. They were dependent on it, they were protective of it, and they were as afraid of it, as they were of any of their Bible preachings.

I had an aunt who had drowned in a river. Her name was Eve. I always called her my Aunt Eve but she had been dead for at least fifteen years before I was ever born. She drowned on my mom's eighth birthday.

I had always felt like my aunt was near me. Until I met the gypsy I thought maybe it was because I heard so many stories about her or because of all the pictures of her that were around my grandparents' house.

My grandparents took me to a carnival one night that had set up in a nearby town for the weekend. A lady dressed like a gypsy offered to tell me my fortune. My grandfather wouldn't give me money for it so the lady said she would do it for free. When she held my hand it felt warm and safe. And when she looked into my eyes to tell my fortune her eyes sparkled like in a cartoon. As she slowly and gently pulled my fingers open she said, "You are a very lucky little girl. You will live long because you have a spirit guide who is watching over you. This guide will protect you always and keep you safe."

As I walked away with my grandparents my grandfather said, "These people who travel around are all just charlatans and thieves. And if they are real they're witches. Either way they're only out to do you no good. Why do you think they always have to move from town to town?"

My grandfather believed everyone was out to do you no good though, he even believed their preacher only became a preacher so he could freeload Sunday dinners off his congregation.

I would sometimes ask my mother to tell me how my aunt had died and each time she would I'd feel like I had been there at the Dusky River that afternoon.

"We were all at the river to celebrate—some cousins and neighbors, Mom and Dad, Eve," my mom would begin. "It was around four and everyone was standing around your grandfather, who was churning ice cream and telling stories. Your Aunt Eve was still playing in the river. It was impossible to ever get her out of the water. She was a fish. She could swim better than anyone around, better than most men. She could do everything better than most people. Everyone admired Eve, she was beautiful and smart and untamed. She wasn't like me, doing whatever Mom and Dad told me to do, never wanting to get anyone mad at me. Eve was a rebel, she had her own mind. And the boys, they loved her, they all loved her. Eve would play with them, give them a kiss, make them think she was theirs but she wasn't. That's why she was so wanted. People want other people the same way lawmen want criminals, the ones they care most to catch, the ones they respect and can't get off their minds or out of their blood are the ones who always get away.

"I remember I heard Eve call out but didn't think anything of it. No one else heard her. When Mom was serving the ice cream she realized Eve wasn't around. At first they all just thought she was up to no good but as it got later we all knew something was wrong.

"We searched for her, then Dad called some people to drag the river. They found Eve around midnight. A current had pulled her under and dragged her almost eleven miles from where we were celebrating.

"Everybody told me she had probably gone down much later than when I heard her call, that she wouldn't have had time to say anything. But I know things would have been different if I looked over then. Of course, I guess we all thought things would've been different if only we had done something other than what we had done. And I don't think that Mom ever forgave herself for believing Eve was doing something bad with boys as she was struggling to stay alive.

"But who knows? Maybe it was as well. She was so

---

wild and independent, always teasing boys. Maybe she was saved from something more horrible."

I knew this was something my mom said because my grandparents had told that to her. They were always saying, "It might not seem like it at the moment but all things happen for the best. God had a reason for this."

My grandparents believed one of the reasons God had for making things happen was to pay you back for the bad you had done. My mom had always said that before Eve died they had been a regular family—that my grandfather had smoked tobacco and cussed and that him and my grandmother even drank whiskey sometimes or kissed in public. But that after Eve was gone they never did anything like that again.

My grandmother bought me my first purse. I picked it out of a sale bin at a Ben Franklin dime store. The purse hung over my shoulders to just below my knees. It was tan straw and had big, plastic wildflowers, of all different colors, sewed on the front. I carried it everywhere filled with my most valuable possessions—a rusty can opener, a tiny glass jar of my baby teeth, a periwinkle crayon, an old sun-dried, whitened wishbone and the last picture of my Aunt Eve that had ever been taken. In the picture my Aunt Eve had waist-long braids and you could tell she was tall and thin. Her face was defined and unchildlike, and she wasn't smiling or sad. She was only fourteen when she died but you could see from my picture that she was going to be very beautiful.

·   ·   ·

The nights in Thelma were still and quiet until around midnight, when I'd wake up to the sounds of cars drag-racing up and down the road. Cars full of teenagers—throwing beer cans, smashing liquor bottles, blasting their radios and heckling each other as one carload would speed past another. A morning hardly went by that something dead wasn't laying to the side of the highway, a chicken, a dog or a cat. One time even a horse had been killed. It looked like a broke-open sack of beets and for a week it was all anyone who stopped by would talk about.

But often the highway was our only source of entertainment. Me and my grandpa would sit on the front porch in the afternoon, rocking in the green chairs, and talk for hours. We'd talk about the cars going by, where they were headed or were from. They'd speed by if they were passing through and drive real slow and wave and honk if they were from anywhere around. Sometimes my grandpa would play his harmonica and sing songs from when he was a boy. My favorite song was "The Troubles of Otis Ott." It was about a guy, Otis, running through a field to get away from a bull. He hops over a fence thinking he's safe and there's a mean, growling dog. He runs through the field and hops over another fence and there's a bear and on and on it goes until finally he hops over a fence and there stands his wife with a rolling pin, which is the person Otis was running away from to begin with.

My grandfather would also tell me tales that he believed

would make me beware of strangers, protect me from danger and prepare me for life. He told me about murderers and rapists and people who were made happy by putting cigarettes out on your bare skin. He'd tell me about the war and war atrocities and that how once someone has lived through a war it can become easier for them to be evil. He'd tell me about lonely farmhouse women getting killed or dying and it being so long before they'd be found that their own cats would've eaten the dead ladies' eyeballs out. But his favorite tale of caution—to make sure I would never not be afraid was his version of the Ed Gein story. Everyone I knew—my parents, other adults, other kids, my other grandparents—had their own personalized rendition of Ed Gein. I'd heard Ed Gein horror stories, sung Ed Gein songs and jumped rope to Ed Gein rhymes. I was warned away from caves, old barns and certain people's property by being told Ed Gein lurked there. But I was never as scared of Ed as when my grandfather would tell me about him. He'd light up his pipe and rock back in the chair and prepare himself as though a huge crowd had just settled in front of him. He'd say, "Ed Gein made women trust him by letting them think he was a fool or a mama's boy. He would lure girls up to his house by asking them to cook dinner for him and he'd cook them for dinner instead. That was how he was so smart, by letting so many people think he was stupid. He laughed every time he carved up one of his victims.

"Ed would make lampshades and chairs and coats out

of his favorite women. And when the sheriffs finally went to his house to bring him in, they found a brain and a heart and some potatoes cooking on his stove.

"You see, everyone thinks it's just your big cities you have to be careful in but there are plenty of sick people out here in the country. Ed wasn't just a fluke. The truth is, it's not safe anywhere. Not anywhere on this earth. That's why I tell you these things. I always want you to be careful because there are more people out there like Eddie than anyone cares to know."

ONE DAY WHEN ME and my grandfather were sitting on the porch a man and woman pulled in the drive. People were always pulling into the half-moon gravel drive to turn around but these people stopped so we walked up the stone pathway towards them. We figured they needed directions since it didn't seem likely my grandfather knew anyone who drove a convertible other than my dad.

The car was the color of a sky-blue Popsicle and it had white seats. The steering wheel looked like a big blue pearl, if a pearl could be cut into the shape of a steering wheel. The lady had long pink fingernails like my mother's and was holding a bottle of strawberry Nehi with one hand and clicking her nails against it with the other. It sounded like gum popping. The man got out of the driver's side and walked around the car, tucking his shirt into his pants the whole time. He walked over and leaned up near where the woman was sitting. Still tucking in his shirt he looked down at me and said, "You must be Will and Phaera's girl. You look like a Groves, that's for sure."

We didn't say anything as the man reached his hand out of his belt loop to shake my grandfather's hand.

"Hey, Mr. Laney. I'm a friend of your daughter. I grew up with this little one's daddy," the man said as he reached over and scuffed his hand across the top of my head. "We were just passing through on the way down to Sugarbluff and remembered that Will told us his girl was staying with you all. We just wanted to say hey to her, get a look at her. Here, we got a little something for you."

The lady reached under the seat and handed me a brown paper sack and said, "Here you go, honey, I picked it out myself."

Inside the bag was a pink plastic vanity set—mirror, comb, brush. The cardboard it was stapled to had pictures of girls with curly hair and jewels. Deeper in the bag was a polka-dotted tube of lipstick with a mirror on the top so you could see to put it on. It was called Candy Kisses and it was bright red-pink in the tube but wouldn't make any color on my lips and it smelled and tasted like strawberries. The lady said, "Well what do you think, sugar? Right color for you?"

"It's the same color as my mom wears. Thanks," I said, licking my lips to taste the strawberry flavor.

I could feel that my grandfather wasn't too crazy about

these people but I thought they were just like my parents. The guy talked to my grandfather awhile about what line of work he was in, who all he had seen lately and what my parents were up to.

"I helped Will paint their house the other weekend. Phaera picked out a real nice color of yellow."

"Just like sunshine," the lady said from the car.

"And they've really fixed up the babies' room," the man said.

It felt strange to me hearing news about my parents, knowing these people I had never seen before knew my mom and dad and little sister better than I did. I wondered if the only way I would ever know about my parents would be from people who would drive through town and stop to tell me new things about their life.

Finally my grandfather asked if they wanted to stay for supper, but anyone would have known he'd have rather gone without five dinners than have them for one. I begged them to say yes but they said they had stayed too long already.

After he got back in his car the man asked, "By the way, you got a liquor store in this town?" My grandfather told him to follow the curve and look to the right as they slowly pulled out the drive. You knew if we hadn't been there they would've peeled out and left a lot of dust.

Back on the porch my grandfather took my bag of presents and started looking through it for the price tags. He pulled a receipt out and held it away from his face to

read, "Two fifty-nine. That's a lot of money to spend on
someone you never met before. Well I guess they oughta
spend what they have fast. They'll kill themselves before
they hit Arkansas."

Arkansas was only about five hundred yards from
where we were sitting. For almost an hour I listened for
car wreck sounds. So far cars had killed about anything
I had ever seen that was dead. I kept seeing their sky-blue
car all crumpled up, the lady's white hair spilled across
the seat, her fingernails broken in little pink chips by the
door, mixed with blood and shattered glass. But I kept
confusing the image of the lady with visions of my mom
in the car instead.

It was a week later that my parents came to take me
home with them for good. My grandmother cut a bouquet of my favorite flowers for me to take. My grandfather hugged me and said to remember all the things he
had told me. Standing by my parents' car waiting to leave,
I told my mom and dad about their friends who had
stopped by and I showed off what they had given me.
My dad started laughing and said that must've been the
same day they totaled out their car. He said, "Brand-new
car. I heard it was crumpled up like a milk carton, but
they didn't get a scratch on them. Some miracle. And
your mom was poutin' all day because she had wanted
to ride to Sugarbluff with them and I wouldn't let her.
Saved the ol' gal's life again."

"Yea. He's saving my life so he can work me to death,"
my mom said as she hugged my dad.

Then we all got in the car and waved goodbye and blew kisses to my grandparents.

This is what I had wished for every night before I went to sleep, to live with my mom and dad and Angie. But now that it was happening I only wanted to run out of their car, back into the only bed I had known as mine. Ever after that time it felt to me like the place I was at was never the place I should be.

When I moved in with my parents I didn't have to go to church anymore. My dad didn't like it because he thought it was just a scheme to get your money and my mom didn't believe in it because she said God had never given her anything she wanted.

Going to church had been one of the things I hated most about living with my grandparents. Every Sunday I heard how we were all doomed to suffer the eternal flames of damnation because we were conceived in sin. The idea of being punished for something that wasn't my fault wasn't new to me, but to pay for it for all eternity— and when you're a kid even one day feels like an eternity— seemed unfair.

The preacher would tell us we had to beg for mercy and admit we were miserable failures every day with hope that the Lord would see fit to forgive and redeem our souls. But if he decided not to see fit and made us burn in hell instead, we were supposed to suffer gratefully. Even though I didn't understand why it mattered what you did at that point.

On the bulletin board at the church were drawings that showed people roasting in hell on turning spits or swimming in seas of fire, their faces twisted in agony and their arms reaching out to be saved. It showed the devil—who looked like the guy on cans of Underwood deviled ham—drinking a big glass of ice water and walking around poking everyone with his pitchfork to make sure they felt terrible enough.

Next to that picture was one of heaven. It was surrounded by beautiful golden gates. Blond, white-winged angels played harps and walked around on gold-paved streets or sat with God, who had long, white flowing hair, a long, white flowing beard and long, white flowing robes. Even though you could tell from the pictures that all the angels were talking to one another I could never imagine what there would be to talk about in heaven if you couldn't talk about anything bad.

You were definitely not allowed to get into heaven if you smoked, drank, looked at women if you were a man, let men look at you if you were a woman, enjoyed sex or had it for more reasons than to have kids. And you couldn't cuss or use the Lord's name in vain. These were things I had looked forward to doing and things my parents did on a regular basis. I'd pray to God a lot to forgive us all for our sinning.

When I moved in with my parents I traded church for school. I soon found out that church was a holiday compared to school.

Kindergarten and my kindergarten teacher, Mrs. Lemmon, were the downfall of my education. The only thing I learned during that year of my life was what the word "exception" meant. On my fourth day of school I had worn a pair of high heels to class. I didn't wear them on purpose, I had been playing in them when my ride came and I didn't think I'd have time to change into my real shoes. When I walked into the school the boys laughed at me and the girls admired my shoes. They were toy high heels but they were as fancy as any ladies' evening shoes. They had black elastic straps across the foot and gold glitter sparkling through the clear plastic heels. Even though they fit my feet they were really hard to walk in. As soon as Mrs. Lemmon noticed my shoes she said, "Since you insisted on wearing these to school I insist you wear them all day long. I don't want to see them off your feet once. And don't think the playground is an exception."

For the whole first recess I played on the swings. Mrs. Lemmon shot me dirty looks every time she looked over and saw that I was having fun.

After lunch, when it was time to carry our chairs to the center of the room to read our *Weekly Readers*, one of the boys offered to carry my chair. Mrs. Lemmon screamed across the room, "Todd Browning, put down that chair. Miss Groves wore those shoes to draw attention to herself. Let her draw attention to herself by letting us all see how foolish a person looks walking in shoes like that."

When I wobbled to the reading circle in my shoes, my ankles kept turning and I almost fell over. A couple of the kids snickered but most of them just kept their heads bowed until I sat down. Then Mrs. Lemmon made me read the opening paragraph.

"Polar bears live very far away where there is only snow and ice. Their paws are as big as a man's head. They are smart and strong and can be ferocious." As I read out loud my voice cracked and I had to try hard to keep from crying. After my turn I spent the rest of the day fantasizing that I had a pet polar bear who I would bring to school with me. It would growl and chase Mrs. Lemmon around while she begged me to forgive her, but I wouldn't. All the kids would laugh and applaud as we watched my polar bear eat her alive. Then we'd do whatever we wanted for the rest of the day.

Mrs. Lemmon was always sending notes home with me saying I didn't follow rules or pay attention. It upset my mom that Mrs. Lemmon disliked me so much. She was afraid that I was going to be one of those kids that people just didn't respond to well. My mom couldn't see it wasn't that people didn't like me, it was that teachers didn't.

I learned there was a big difference between people and teachers, but there was hardly any difference between teachers and parents. Both relied on placation, deception and control—mostly control—to get what they wanted.

Parents and teachers were allied by a common bond— they hated their jobs and each believed it was the other one's fault their job was so awful. I was kind of an authority on this subject since I not only had parents and teachers I also had a parent who was a teacher.

My mom cared a lot about the kind of impression I made in school because she was an elementary-grade teacher. She told me my behavior was a reflection on what kind of teacher she was. One evening my first grade had given a square dance performance for the parents of the whole school. While all the kids clapped and stood in formation waiting to do-si-do, I sat down on the floor cross-legged until my partner danced up to me. After the show my mom rushed me and my dad and Angie out to the car. As soon as the doors were closed my mom started in, "How could you have done that to me? You humiliated me. None of the other children did anything to embarrass their parents." She had begun crying by this point. "They all stood up straight and did their steps and there you were sitting on the floor, like the whole show was just for you. How do you think that makes me look? You don't care about me at all. What was wrong with you?"

"My legs were tired," I said.

My mom looked at me like she hadn't been crying at all. As she turned her back to me, she snapped, "No, they weren't."

The next day my mom wore sunglasses when we came to school and ever after that time she would do her best to make whatever school projects I had the best one.

In second grade my class was chosen to sing Christmas

carols at a department store. I had wanted to play the recorder with the other kids but my teacher, Mrs. Atkins, told me I didn't follow directions good enough. She made me play the triangle, which meant I had to stand in the back row, where no one would see me.

For the occasion my mom stayed up three nights in a row sewing me a special Christmas skirt by hand. It was red velvet and had raised bells made of silver sequins, a Christmas tree of green sequins with some red and gold sequins for ornaments, a sequined Santa's sleigh and "Merry Christmas" spelled out in all different colors of sequins. It was the most beautiful skirt in the world and I would keep it hanging on my bedroom doorknob just so I could fall asleep looking at it.

The night the class met at the department store to perform, Mrs. Atkins was handing out our instruments when the store manager came over and told her the local news station was going to put us on TV. All the kids and the parents were excited as Mrs. Atkins started arranging our places. She walked over to hand me my triangle and said, "Back row, third from left."

A man from the TV station walked up and took my hand. He didn't look at Mrs. Atkins. "You. Right up here in the front, little lady. You look just like a holiday. We want you in special view because of that fancy skirt you have on."

My mom was close enough to hear the man and I watched her smiling.

"My mom made it," I told the man as I pointed my mom out.

"Well your skirt is almost as pretty as your mom," he answered, centering me in front of the rest of the class.

Mrs. Atkins wasn't too happy how things turned out that night but my mom told me she had never been more proud. I felt really good until I figured it was mostly the skirt she was proud of.

———————

AT THE BEGINNING of every summer vacation my mom would give me and Angie a Children's Day. She'd say, "There's a Mother's Day and Father's Day, so we have to have a Children's Day." We got to pick whatever we wanted to do on that day. We'd eat what we wanted, buy what we wanted and go where we wanted. I always picked to go to my grandparents', buy paper dolls and eat a What-A-Burger. Angie would go along with my choices.

One Children's Day there was a semi-truck parked in front of the What-A-Burger stand. Painted on the side of the trailer were pictures of elephant-size rats. A man stood out front with a microphone describing the giant man-eating rats he had caged inside and saying they had actually been reported to have eaten alive soldiers in the

Civil War. I wanted to go inside but my mom said they were fake and it would be a waste of money. She ended up letting me go but I had to go in alone. When I walked through the trailer I saw three live animals that looked like gerbils the size of small pigs. The whole time a tape played telling how vicious the rats were and not to let them see you looking at them or they would try to escape and attack you. The rats didn't look up at me once, they just kept eating the wilted lettuce that was strewn around their cage.

Normally it seemed like people were conned into thinking something was nice that was really bad. I had never experienced the opposite of that before.

When I walked out of the trailer my mom asked, "Well, how was it? Did they try to eat you up?"

"No. They didn't even hardly move," I said disappointedly.

"What a gyp," Angie said.

"Yea, I know."

"Well maybe next time you'll realize that occasionally I know what I'm talking about," my mom said.

"I just wanted to see for myself," I answered.

"Hmm . . . Only a fool learns from experience," my mom said. I wished that she would find a new expression someday.

Not long after that Children's Day—which turned out to be our last one—I ran away from home. One morning me and Angie were playing some board game. Angie started cheating like she always did because I was winning, like I always did. We ended up in a pinching, scratching, crying match. My mom ran into the living room and screamed, "Stop it! I can't stand this anymore. That's all you girls do is fight." Then she kicked the board so that it went up in the air and the pieces flew all over.

Angie looked at my mom like she was the Creature still covered with lake moss and cried, "You almost poked my eye out."

She was still too young to know you can never use the same lines adults use on you, so she was unprepared for the back of my mom's hand when it came. I tried to grab Angie away from my mom but she yanked me back, then grabbed our arms and dragged us down the hall into our rooms.

"Stay in there," she yelled as she slammed our doors shut. I think my parents must have realized early on that me and Angie were more powerful together and that was why we had separate rooms across the hall from one another. I also think that's why they never had more kids.

I was so mad at my mom for hitting Angie and sending us to our rooms I decided to show her and leave home for good. I packed a set of pajamas and a sweater in my overnight bag that was shaped like a clown's head and put on my favorite T-shirt. It was one of my dad's rejects, it had wide, bright orange and white stripes and came to my knees. I looked around my room to say goodbye to all my things, then opened my bedroom window. I threw my overnight bag out and grabbed the Bible my grandparents had given me that I kept on my nightstand. I threw it carefully so it would land on the bag, then crawled out the window.

I couldn't even think of how far I'd get or any other specifics, all I could think about was how sorry my mom would feel for what she had done when she opened my door and saw I had left.

It was only about ten in the morning and the sun was real bright. I knew I wouldn't feel safe until I was off our street but the closer I got to the end of the block the harder my heart pounded. At the corner of Lone Pine and Sequiota I decided to pick a direction. My only choice was my best friend Anne Rozwell's house or the railroad tracks. I had played on the railroad tracks for years. All the kids had stories about following them to Arkansas or Oklahoma but everyone knew they were really only crosstown tracks.

Springfield was a small city that was surrounded by even smaller, time-warped towns and within four hours of two major American cities. It was inhabited by the type of people who had left their big-city homes to escape crime, dirt, bad schools and traffic, or those who had moved from smaller places to escape crime, boredom, bad schools and isolation. Regardless of where they are from originally, people who converge on a medium-population town are a lot alike. Above all else they value safety, comfort and convenience.

Springfield was segregated by directions—the south was rich and liberal, west was poor whites, east was working middle class, the north side was blacks and the far north were the Southern Baptists, the fundamentalists and evangelists. We lived on the south side but we weren't rich. We were part of the borderliners, the people who lived in smaller houses on the entrance streets to the heart of the south side. This was a constant source of humiliation for my mother, and every time she would have to give out our address her voice would get harder to hear.

Rarely did southsiders go to the north side, which seemed too mysterious, the east, which was boring, or the west part of town, which had the reputation for being scary and violent. It was the same for everyone—except wild teenagers who didn't adhere to any boundaries of where to be. So going crosstown, especially by the railroad tracks, was about as foreign as going to another state. I settled for going to Anne's house.

Me and Anne Rozwell had talked about running away together ever since first grade, after we'd read *The Boxcar Children*. Feeling like The Fugitive, I took the back roads to Anne's house and before I went up to her door I hid my night bag and Bible under their shrubs in case her mom answered, which she did. I asked if Anne was home.

"It's kind of early isn't it, honey? Everything all right?" her mom asked.

"Yea," I answered, wondering why she was asking. It killed me how every time something was a little out of the ordinary parents automatically believed you had done something they were going to have to rot in prison for.

"Well come on in, she's cleaning her room."

"I'll wait out here," I said, looking down at my shoes.

When Anne's mom went inside I started getting butterflies. I wondered if she knew what I was doing and was going to call the police.

Anne finally came to the door and I told her what had happened and reminded her how we had planned to run away together. Tears started in my eyes as I said, "Today is the day we're doing it." Suddenly all I could see was my mom's face when she was being nice to me or bringing me food.

Anne said, "Are you sure? You don't look too sure."

"I already did it. Come on."

"But I'll get in trouble. You were already in trouble so it doesn't matter for you."

"That's not true. Besides we're leaving. What can they do to you when you're not there?"

Anne was doing what she always did. She was the one who had come up with the idea of running away to begin with, saying, "We'll be just like the Boxcar Children, we'll go wherever we want, stay up however late we want and build a house in the woods." But now that I had gone and done it, it wasn't such a great idea for her.

I had known Anne since kindergarten and we had always been close friends. Actually she was my closest friend but not the one I liked best. I was close to Anne because her family was the only one I visited that didn't make me feel like there was something wrong with my own family.

"Well what will we eat?" Anne whined.

"Nuts and berries or we can steal stuff from bakeries, like in the book."

"There aren't any bakeries around here. Besides, how will we know which berries are poisonous?"

"I don't know, just c'mon."

Anne stalled around, picking the blue buds off the sticker bush she was standing by. "These are poisonous. You can die instantly from these."

"I know. Are you coming or what?" I asked.

"OK," Anne said, "I'll go pack." Anne told her mom instead.

As Anne's mom drove me home she kept telling me everything would be all right, that my parents would be so happy to see me they'd forget all about being mad. But I knew she was just trying to make herself feel better for turning me over. Besides, Anne's mom was a divorcée and they were always a lot easier on their kids.

My dad was sitting on the front porch when we pulled in the drive. As I walked up to the house he waved bye to Mrs. Rozwell, then motioned me onto his lap. I started to cry as he pulled me to his chest. My mom came outside. Her eyes were narrow slits and she barely moved her lips as she said, "Thanks a lot, sweetheart."

I had been hoping that running away would make my mom see she should treat me different, that she might get so worried she'd realize how sad she would feel if I was gone for good. But it hadn't worked. Looking up at her made me stop crying.

I fell over a brick wall once and tore a huge gash out of the front of my leg. There was tons of blood and ripped skin. As my mom was doctoring it I kept saying, "I didn't even cry once."

"Bodies can't handle the big hurts, it goes numb so you won't feel all the pain. Only the little cuts can make you cry," she had said, blowing on my knee.

As my mom glared at me my dad covered the side of my head with his hand and rocked me in the chair. "Do you have to be so damn nasty all the time? Leave the girl alone. Why do you think she left in the first place?"

"Well where were you when she took off? If you were raising them alone the way I am it'd be a whole other story."

"Why are you always complaining?" he asked.

"You don't know what I'm always doing. You're never here."

"I know you complain when there's nothing to complain about. I know other women don't complain the way you do."

"Other women have men that stay around the house, that don't take off for days in the woods. Or wherever you go."

"Who the hell would want to stay around here?"

"Well get the hell out then. I don't ask you to stay and I don't ask you to come back. But when you leave this time take your darling daughter with you. You two are one and the same."

My dad stood up out of the rocker with me. "You're a mean, old, woman," he said, making the words "mean" and "old" and "woman" like whole sentences to themselves.

As my dad carried me to his truck I could see tears drop from my mom's eyes. I wanted to jump down from my dad and run over to hold my mom, to tell her I was sorry, to tell her I loved her, that my dad didn't mean what he said, but she turned her back to me and went inside the house.

My dad kept his truck stocked with a gun, a fishing rod, food and clothes so that if he didn't have time to pack his stuff from the house he could still go wherever he wanted, when he wanted. He drove me to three Dairy Queens before we found one that had chocolate ice cream. My dad handed me tons of napkins and made me keep them around the cone in case I let it drip. He said, "Let's go to the lake for a few days."

I said, "Mom didn't mean it. It was mine and Angie's fault to begin with. Let's just go home."

"Ah, we can't go home now. The ol' squaw will just hound us for leaving to start with."

"She won't for long if you'll be nice to her."

"There's no being nice to her," my dad said. "She's just like her ol' man. He is always bitchin' too."

I couldn't recall most of the things my dad told me

about my grandparents. "I didn't ever hear Granpa yell at Granma," I said to him.

"Well how would you know? You only see 'em once a month. Course they're gonna act OK then," my dad said with a dare in his eyes.

"But they didn't ever fight when I lived there," I answered. Whenever I had talked about living with my grandparents my dad would deny it with such anger I'd be afraid to say any more about it.

"You never lived there," he said now. "We'd let you stay there when you cried to, but only for a few days."

This was the first time my dad had ever said this and sounded so calm and reassuring on the subject. It made me feel safe to say more. "I lived there when I was little. I remember. Mom even said it was true."

"Well she's off her rocker. I've been taking care of you since the day you were born." My dad laughed.

"Where did we live when I was a baby?"

"Together."

"But where? What house?"

"Finish up that cone before it melts all over the seat," my dad said, sounding impatient.

I started licking my ice cream faster. "How come Mom tells me I lived in Thelma?" I asked.

Really the only time my mom told me straight out I had lived with my grandparents was after a bad fight her and my dad had. When he left the house my mom said, "He's a worthless man. That's why you had to live with

Mom and Dad for so long because your own father didn't want to take care of you."

But other than that one time she acted the same way my dad did whenever I'd talk about living there.

"When did she tell you that?"

"Lots of times," I lied.

"Well she's crazy. You didn't live there and I don't want to ever hear about it again. You must be getting just as crazy as she is."

I had seen on a TV show someone once say, "One sign a person is crazy is when they have no idea they are crazy. Of course, some of the insane are insane by the knowledge of their own insanity." I sat there wondering if it would be better for me to take after my mom and believe I was crazy, or if I should be like my dad and keep convinced that I wasn't.

We ended up driving to The Cat and the Fiddle, the bar my dad drank beer and played pool in. The Cat and the Fiddle was on one of the busiest strips in town but had mostly a regular clientele. Just about everyone there knew me and my dad when we'd go in. Sometimes I'd even go in after school with a friend and order Cokes for us and put them on my dad's tab. It was always dark inside the bar, too cold in the summer and too warm in the winter.

Between the lounge and the highway, at the top of a

big steel pole was a black, dancing neon cat playing a fiddle. Each time the neon blinked black and red and purple the cat looked like it was stepping to a tune. I spent a lot of time waiting in the car for my dad if he wasn't in the mood for me to be in the bar with him and I would stare at the neon cat. It was spooky the way it seemed like it was winking at you no matter where you were from it.

One night when I was waiting for my dad to come out I watched a woman drive a brand-new Lincoln Continental through the front window of the bar. She stepped out of the car like nothing had even touched her, broken glass falling out of her hair. She was carrying a fireplace log and I could see her smash all the bottles of liquor behind the bar that hadn't been broken in the crash. Then a man ran through the now open bar window. The woman was running after him screaming, with the log still raised above her head. All I could think of, as I watched my dad and three other men standing in the rubble and laughing, was the song my grandfather used to sing of Otis Ott.

That afternoon as we pulled into the parking lot I saw three cars I recognized and Cliff Wyatt's GMC pickup, that my dad always made fun of. I knew it was going to be a long day. We stayed until eleven that night. When we got home my mom and Angie were already in bed.

I couldn't sleep the whole night wondering what my

mom would say to me in the morning but she didn't say anything to me for the next two days.

———————

WHENEVER MY DAD would get mad at me he would say I was crazy just like my mom. When my mom was mad at me she said I was my dad all over again. When my mom was really mad at me she would tell me I was just like my Aunt Louise. My mom said my Aunt Louise was one of those women who got through life strictly from having the fortune of being born with good looks and bad morals. She was my dad's sister and there were a few things I could count on every time she would come to visit. She would be with a new man, she'd have a new color of hair, my mom and dad would fight for at least a day afterward, and she would always take me someplace special.

Once she took me to see Tammy Wynette sing. My aunt was a big fan of Tammy Wynette's and every time she'd hear her come on the radio she would say, "A voice like hers is cut from sheer heartache. That lady knows all there is to know about love."

Louise had gotten free tickets from a roadie who had a crush on her. The roadie had met my aunt at a bar the night before and promised to introduce her to Tammy

Wynette after the show. As we walked to our seats the roadie spotted us. He jumped off the stage and pulled us up to the front row. "I scored these two places for you. You're in the VIP section," he blurted out. Then the man tried to kiss my aunt on the lips but she saw it coming and at that moment she turned toward me. He ended up banging his mouth clumsily against the side of her face. The man turned red and mumbled, "Well enjoy yourselves. I'll come get you after the show." As he walked away my aunt said, "Don't you go away from my side. You're my protection tonight."

Aunt Louise wouldn't do a thing for any guy unless he was rich but she would let any guy do all they could for her. But as beautiful as my Aunt Louise was she never had a good-looking man. They were all overweight, over six feet tall, kind of bald and had pink, rashy skin.

One day we heard a horn honking in our driveway. I ran to the window and saw Louise cuddled up to a man sitting behind the steering wheel of a long, lavender Cadillac convertible. I yelled for Angie and we followed my parents out to the drive. My mom was wiping flour off her hands onto an apron. She said, "You must know every time I'm at my worst because that's the only time you drop by."

"Well love, your worst is most people's best," Louise said. "Now look at my brother, didn't I tell you he was the most handsome man alive?" she said, pointing to my dad, then she took the white glove she was holding and slapped the man in the belly with it.

"Sure does run in the family," the man said.

"Now we don't even have time to get out of my brand-new car, kids. I just had to make Gilbert drive me by here to show off. What do you think, Willy?"

"What the hell color is it, Lou?" my dad asked laughing.

"Lilac, it's a custom color," Louise answered.

My mom was being friendly but I could tell she was going to be mad when my aunt left. I was just hoping they wouldn't get out of the car because I had learned that the longer my mom had to fake being happy when she wasn't, the madder she got and the longer it lasted.

"It looks like a big flower. Say, Gilbert, don't you feel silly driving that thing around?" my dad asked as he laughed harder.

"Not as long as Louise is here by my side," Gilbert answered.

"Isn't he a dream? He gave me this little flower, by the way." Louise caressed her hands across the dashboard, then squeezed the man around his neck.

My mom bristled. Half the fights I had heard her and my dad have over my aunt were how she always got fancy presents from men. I didn't know why it bothered my mom that men liked my aunt so much. Then my mom said, "Well Louise, that sure is a nice gift. What's the occasion?"

"Now I don't know. Gilbert, you didn't tell me what the occasion was?"

"Every day with Louise is an occasion." He grinned.

Louise snuggled into him again, then said, "Back out, Gil. It's time to get on the road. We're going to St. Louis. Gil's taking me to the zoo."

We all waved and ran our hands along the side of the car as Gilbert backed out of the drive. Louise was smiling and waving like she was riding a float in a beauty parade.

"What kind of fool would buy a car like that for a woman who can't even drive?" my dad said as he slapped my mom on the butt.

Since my dad was unimpressed my mom didn't get mad at all.

I guess I had felt so nervous the whole time we were all standing by the Cadillac, that when my mom put her arm over my shoulder as we walked in the house I started to cry. Gilbert was the grossest man yet I had seen my aunt with. He wore black horn-rimmed glasses and had thin, greasy black hair, combed over to cover a shiny bald spot. His face was oily and long hairs grew out of his nose and ears. He wasn't fat but he looked soft and limp. And as he had waved goodbye I saw that he had long, tapered fingernails.

My mom looked down at me with surprise. "What on earth's the matter?" she asked.

"Why do you always tell me I'm going to end up like Aunt Louise?" I cried, gasping and wiping away my tears.

My mom lifted me up with a groan and locked my

legs around her waist, laughing as she said, "Sometimes I say that because your aunt is an example of what happens if you only think about boys. But don't worry, Misty, I love you much too much to let that happen to you."

———————————

THE FIRST BOY I fell in love with was a boy I saw on TV. It was Sunday night and me and my mom and sister were watching Walt Disney. That night it was about this boy, Johnny Tremain, who fought in the American Revolution. He had dark hair, was quiet, and was the hero. Every time Johnny Tremain spoke or moved I felt pains in my stomach from being able to see him so clear and not be able to touch him. I don't remember if it was just because the show was over or if Johnny Tremain had died, but for days after that movie I cried. At first my mom tried to reason with me. She'd tell me that it was only a movie or that there were lots of cute boys in our town. Then she tried logic, saying, "You're only five, he's at least a teenager. By the time you'd be old enough to marry him he'd be an old man and possibly even bald. Besides, you have to be on TV to meet people who are on TV." Finally she used threats. She said if I didn't dry my eyes by the next day she would take me to a doctor and have him give me shots. So I stopped crying. I hated shots, especially when I knew they wouldn't cure me.

My mom believed that I had a preoccupation with boys. That it was something I had brought into life with me, that I had asked, out of vengefulness to her, whoever hands out attributes for this particular one. What she didn't want to realize was that like everything else that's wrong with you in life it was my parents' fault to begin with that I ever had this problem. And to make it even worse my parents had named me Misty.

I tried to change my name once after I had watched an episode of *Laredo* on TV. It was about a young girl named Dixie who had run away from an orphanage to seek revenge on the man who had murdered her parents. Even though Dixie didn't sound so different from Misty, in meaning it was a whole other person. She was tough, not afraid of anything, and she didn't care about boys.

The Texas Rangers had found Dixie and were bringing her back, against her will, to the orphanage. Sitting by the campfire one night Dixie started talking to the Ranger who was guarding her. "Seems like you all would have bigger criminals to go after than me. Or are you guys too old to be sent after anyone who's really dangerous?"

The Ranger who was guarding her was the sourest of the three. He was old and scruffy and hard-acting, but you knew he really loved Dixie. He reminded me of my grandfather. To whatever Dixie would say the old Ranger would reply, "Hmpf. We'll get you into a dress. That will change your airs."

"Well if you old scarecrows think buying me a dress

to wear is gonna make me be different then you're all senile. I'll just run off again."

"You'll never be able to get a man to take care of you if you don't learn how to girl yourself up a bit, missy," the Ranger said. "And since I'm not going to spend the rest of my years running after you, a man is just what you need."

In a voice affected to sound like a grown-up woman's, she said, "I'm not interested in men. I don't care if I ever find one to be with. The only reason I even look at them is to study them, learn their ways, so they can't trap me."

When the show ended I told my parents and my sister to call me Dixie from now on. Angie was the only one who would but every time she did she'd laugh so hard it didn't count. I vowed not to leave my room until my parents said I could change my name in a court of law.

After about three hours my mom came in my room.

"Can I change my name?" I asked.

My mom sat down on the bed, she put her hands on my head to brush the hair away from my face. My mom's fingernails were always long and painted a color of beige or pink, she had big hands and long, narrow fingers that were soft and would fold to whatever part of your body they were against. My mom said, "When you were born and I first looked at you, you were so helpless and needed me so much it made me misty. I love you more than you'll ever know. I named you Misty because that's how you made me feel and that's how I still feel every time I look at you."

This was my mom's trademark, being able to make it sound like every mistake she made wasn't a mistake at all but something she did because she loved you so much. I figured I was stuck with my name until I was at least sixteen.

BY THIRD GRADE IT had become apparent to my mom that school and boys would continue to be a problem for me. Taking hints from all the modern magazines on child psychology, my mom started to believe it was best to not fight my aberration and began to incorporate boys into my training. Like giving a horse sugar. Thinking it would make me more conscientious about my school-work, she told me boys had more respect for girls who made good grades. This backfired because I still wouldn't do better in school so I started to like the kind of boys who didn't care if you were on the honor roll—and became especially infatuated with those boys who considered it a handicap.

My mom would say to me, "Misty, boys don't like girls who are boy-crazy, even the troublemakers. Look at Lynn Mason. She's popular with all the boys, they respect her. She makes A's and doesn't chase them around." I knew my mom wished she could ask Mrs. Mason to trade her Lynn for me. It seemed like every day I heard "Lynn Mason this . . ." or "Lynn Mason that. . . ."

Lynn had been in school with me since first grade and all the teachers and my mom used her for an example of how to behave. All the girls wanted to be her best friend and all the boys were in love with her. She never made an effort to be so sought after, she just was. My mom used to tell me that was because Lynn had "it." She would say, "Most famous people have 'it' and that's how they get famous to begin with. You don't need money, brains, or good looks if you've got 'it.' "

I would try to pinpoint my mom on what this "it" was but all she would tell me was "it" couldn't be defined, acquired or learned, it was just a certain something you were born with that made people want to be around you.

Lynn Mason was the closest I ever got to having a science project. If I could've gotten away with it I would've entered her as my exhibit in the annual science fair.

EXPERIMENT: Why Lynn Mason Is So Popular.
HYPOTHESIS: Because her dad is a doctor, they belong to a country club, and she's the only girl in a family of three brothers.
DATA: Lynn Mason is consistently the only girl allowed to play softball. When it is time to line up to go inside Lynn walks to the line and is followed by at least two boys talking to her about softball plays. Lynn always does best in gym class, she outlasts even

the boys in the bent-arm hang and does more push-ups than the teacher will count. She's good at bat, she only wears madras or solid-color clothes. She laughs easy and loud but not so loud as Cathy Whistle. She brings her lunch in a Granite-man lunch pail and she drinks a lot of milk.

I hated milk. I didn't laugh so easy. I liked dresses with flowers or pastel stripes. I was good at sports but not as good as Lynn. And I carried a Bonanza lunch pail. I secretly loved it because there was a picture of Little Joe on the front and I wanted to marry him when I got older. But all the kids made fun of it. My dad had found the lunch box in an old abandoned house. It was rusty and beat-up and had a leather strap instead of a plastic handle like all the new lunch boxes that were lined up in the coat room. And worst of all, it didn't have a Thermos. With all this data I came to the conclusion that Lynn Mason was so popular because she was completely unaware of the notion that there were two sexes.

Of course, it took me almost a year to reach my conclusion since most of my research could only be logged during recess. And even while I felt very single-minded in my efforts to study Lynn, I'd usually get sidetracked and develop a crush on one of the guys instead.

One day I fell in love with Raymond Edmunds. It was really hot that day. He was being catcher and instead of kneeling in position behind the batter he was lying on his side, really bored. His head was propped on one hand and his other arm was resting across his hip and bent so that his glove was up and open. The batter hit a foul pop fly and Raymond didn't move when the ball came at him except to barely tip his mitt. He caught the fly. Everyone was too shocked to react at the moment but for the whole rest of the school year Raymond was treated like he was the son of some famous manly movie star.

The next year Raymond and I were in the same class again and he still didn't know I existed until one morning during show and tell.

Over the weekend my dad and I had gone to the river. A tree half connected to its trunk had broken and was bobbing on the water. An owl was perched on one of the thicker branches. Me and my dad were standing on one side of the river, close enough that the owl should have been scared off. My dad said, "I want to see the wing span on that thing," and he started throwing rocks near the owl so we could watch it fly away, but it didn't move. Then my dad grabbed a long, broken-off branch and jabbed at the owl. He poked the chest of the bird with the tip of the branch, then said, "It's dead all right. It's got a death grip on that tree. There's no way to move something when it's got a death grip." We tried to figure out how it could've died and my dad said it had probably been struck by lightning. Before we left the river my dad waded over to the tree, took out his knife and cut just above the owl's claw. The owl still stood the same as if he had two claws. That night my dad tied strings to the tendons of the claw he had cut off, and when you pulled the strings the claw would open or close.

I took the claw to show and tell with me the next day and after my turn I passed it around. All the guys in class and Lynn Mason thought it was really neat. The other girls refused to touch it. By lunchtime word had gotten around about my claw and almost every boy in school wanted to see it and a few of them tried offering me five or six dollars for it.

At the end of the day Raymond Edmunds came up and asked if he could walk me home. I was too in love with him to speak but every time he'd catch me looking at him he'd smile at me. Before we got to my house I gave him the claw for keeps. He said, "Thanks," and when he looked in the brown paper bag to see it again he said, "This is really great. Well, I'll see ya tomorrow." Raymond never asked to walk me home again. I think I learned a lesson from that, but I still don't know if it was one that made me be smarter or dumber with boys.

One of the things I did learn from Raymond and from the owl's claw was that boys like dead things and animal parts. This was something I could get a steady supply of.

My dad was a sportsman, he hunted and fished every day, and every night I watched him clean quail or squirrel, rabbits, pheasants, fish, deer, whatever was in season. My dad cleaned the fish at the kitchen sink. Sometimes a fish wouldn't be dead yet and he'd conk it on top of its head with a knife handle. When he killed a deer he would drag it into the basement by its antlers and hang it to pulleys that were attached to rafters. The deer hung upside down and was cut in certain places—behind the knee bones where the scent glands had been removed and across the throat to bleed it. My parents saved newspapers and this was what my dad cleaned all the animals on or over. There is a certain smell when blood and fresh meat, feathers or fur mix with newsprint. I would stare in the eyeballs of the things my dad was cleaning and no matter how dead their bodies looked, their eyes never looked like they were empty yet. It seemed like every different kind of animal saw whatever they were seeing in a different kind of way.

Once after my dad had been frog gigging I asked if he would wait until I invited a friend over before he cleaned them. I called Russ Baker, who lived two houses up the road from us. Russ wasn't your cutest-boy-in-class type. He was kind of scraggly and scrawny. He had long hair that looked like he cut it himself and always wore clothes that looked like he had picked them out because they were the easiest thing in his closet to grab. Russ would take me out on his mini-bike sometimes and I was in love with him. As soon as I heard his mini-bike pull up the drive I went out and took him in the garage to watch my dad. He let Russ clean a frog himself, then invited him to stay for supper. My dad said, "I'll fix it so the legs jump in the skillet." I knew this would make Russ like me more but my mom would like me less—figuring I was in on the scheme. I said to my dad, "We better tell Mom first. You know it makes her sick to see them wiggle." My dad winked at Russ and said, "Watching the frogs jump is only half the fun." Him and Russ laughed.

When we walked in the kitchen my dad told my mom that Russ was eating with us. Everything was nice, my dad offered Russ a beer and poured him a Coke and my sister didn't talk at all. My mom breaded the legs while I set the table. I kept looking at my mom, trying to signal her in on the legs by making my eyes look like they were popping but she'd just smile at me then move her lips to say, "Yes, he's cute." My mom put the legs in the skillet and as soon as they began twitching she started screaming.

"Why do you do this to me? I tell you every time, I'll cook the damn things but make them so they'll lay still. You don't care about me at all, you never have."

"They're dead. What's the big deal?" My dad asked. But my dad knew what the big deal was.

My mom was always talking about wanting to live in a penthouse apartment in Paris or New York City. She had wanted to be a stewardess or model or an interior decorator, not something common like a teacher. Cooking the jumping frog legs made my mom feel like she lived on a farm in Thelma, it made her see how near she still was to the place she had wanted to escape from.

"You'll never understand me. You'll never just be nice. I hate you for this." My mom had tears in her eyes.

My dad laughed and said, "For God's sake, Phae, we got company."

My mom slammed a plate of sliced tomatoes down on the table and yelled, "Well you wanted to put on a show. Here it is."

My sister got up from the table and walked into the family room and turned on the TV. My dad grabbed the cooking tongs, saying, "Why you've gone half crazy. Are you drunk?"

That stopped my mom cold and she answered, "You do something to deliberately get me upset. In front of the girls' friend. Then you call me names? You goddamn sonofabitch."

As me and Russ stared in the frying pan at the legs popping around, my mom stormed out of the kitchen and slammed the door to the bathroom so hard the house rattled.

My dad fixed me and Russ two plates of frog legs and we went on to the porch to eat. Russ said, "I can't believe your mom cusses." I hated her until he said, "That's pretty cool." The whole time we were eating we could hear my parents fighting and throwing things. Listening to my parents made me tired, my whole body seemed to fall closer to the ground and even the frog leg was heavy to hold. I felt like I was aging at a phenomenal pace and had never been a kid at all, that I had never been a baby, maybe that I had never even been born but had just popped up in the middle of some field and got thrown where I landed only to be thrown out later on.

This feeling wasn't new except that usually I was alone when it came over me. Having Russ there, though, made it not so lonely. Russ's dad and mom were always fighting too and sometimes his mom would leave for days and no one would know where she was. And even when she wasn't taking off she wasn't around much. When she was home she only watched TV and sat on their couch smoking cigarettes and drinking liquor. Russ looked over at me and said, "It'll be OK, Misty. Parents are always yelling at each other. They'll get over it."

"Yea, but sometimes it takes days before they start being nice to each other again," I said, trying not to cry.

"I know. You just gotta ignore 'em, though."

"I wish I still lived with my granma and grandpa."

"Yea. I wish my granma was still alive. Things were a lot better when she lived with us."

After we finished our food Russ asked me to walk down to the creek. We waded through the water and Russ held my hand and I wanted the creek to be so long we'd be able to wade into another state. Russ kept talking about the frog legs, he said they tasted like fish sticks on a bone. I told him I hadn't ever eaten fish sticks and he said I could come over to his house for dinner next time he cooked them. Russ said his mom wasn't much of a cook. Then he kissed me, not a long kiss but it felt really nice. I wanted to drift in that kiss to a place so far away I'd never have to return to where I had come from. I wished we were vagabonds, sleeping together in abandoned trains and houses every night.

Back then I spent most of my time wishing for something—places I'd rather be, lives I'd rather have. I could lay under a tree and look up through the branches and remember stuff or wish for things until someone came along and made me move for some reason, I could lay by the creek and listen to the water tremble over the rocks until the water ran out.

Every report card I brought home would have written under the CONDUCT AND BEHAVIOR section, "Misty daydreams. She doesn't pay attention in class or on the playground." My mom and dad always made a big deal over this. I guessed that daydreaming upset parents and teachers so much because they wanted to be in charge of everything you thought. Mrs. Atkins once told me that calling a person a daydreamer was just a nicer way of telling them they were lazy. She went on to say that I was the laziest girl she had ever seen and that if she believed in reincarnation she believed I would come back to earth in a wheelchair. I didn't know what reincarnation meant then and I guess I was too lazy to find out but when I did a few years later I got really scared and thought that old woman had a point, but I still couldn't make myself get up and do anything, so it just gave me something else to lay around and think about.

Russ was sent away to live with an aunt and uncle during our sixth-grade year. His mom had gotten put away in a mental institution because one day she got drunk and went to the grocery store naked. Russ had said it was the only time he knew of that she had gone grocery shopping. I wanted Russ to stay and live in his house by himself but he said the authorities wouldn't let him. He said as soon as he turned sixteen he would drive back to be with me. We were young enough to believe that might happen.

Russ sent me one letter. Inside was a picture of a wolf he had torn out of a magazine. The wolf was standing in some short weeds facing the camera. He wasn't stoic, brave or lone-looking, he just seemed skinny and hungry. Russ had drawn a cartoon caption cloud coming from the wolf's mouth and had written inside it, "This is me." I tacked the page on the wall by my bed and every night I would stare at it before I would go to sleep. If Russ had sent me his school picture it wouldn't have reminded me of him as much as the photograph of the wolf did.

MY MOM WAS OFTEN upset by the kind of boys I picked to like. She said they were just like my dad—good-looking, good-for-nothing, and only out for a good time. She would say, "Misty, I want you to do better for yourself than I did. Find the kind of boys who will amount to something—they may not be the most fun to be around, they may not be the sweet talkers, but you won't have to worry about things."

Mrs. Magnus was my mom's prime example of a

woman who married the right kind of man. Mrs. Magnus taught at the same school my mom did. She was big, had stiff, coiffed hair and wore only earth-tone-colored clothes. Her husband was a salesman, not the type that went door to door but the kind who was out of town a lot. My mom thought Mrs. Magnus was lucky because her husband would go shopping with her, help her cook for dinner parties, help her clean the house and visit her friends with her. My dad was always making fun of Mr. Magnus, and when he went to parties with my mom's friends he'd come home talking about what pussies all the husbands were. Even though my mom would get mad at my dad for this it did seem like she took some kind of pride, at least for that little while, in the fact that my dad was who he was. My mom liked it that my dad was handsome and funny, and not fat or old-looking like most of the other husbands she knew. Plus I think she knew my dad did these same things for my mom when she asked him to.

I guess like most girls I fell in love with boys that reminded me of my dad. The only problem was I wasn't sure if they were boys like my dad or boys who were like my mom described my dad. At that age most of the guys I thought I loved were a lot older than me. I would hang out and talk to them while they worked on their cars in their driveways, or sit on the curb and watch while they played basketball at the dead end of our street.

One guy who I fell in love with then was Francis Blue-gill. He called me "Willbe" whenever he saw me. One day I asked him why he called me that and he said, "Because someday you will be a fine-looking thing."

Francis Bluegill had a bad reputation and people said he was dangerous. The people on our block took a kind of pride in the fact that we all dared to live so near the most notorious nineteen-year-old on the south side of Springfield. Local legend had it that Francis only graduated from high school because he threatened to kill the principal if he wasn't allowed to. I had never seen Francis be mean. I had only seen him be calm, like he was thinking about something far away, or joking around and saying things that made everyone laugh.

Francis always wore jeans and a thick leather belt that was tooled with soaring eagles. The belt had a big silver buckle with the word COMANCHE engraved in ornate, bold letters. Francis hardly ever wore a shirt, even on the coldest days. He had a smooth, tan chest and arms that were long and strong and a ponytail that hung straight down the middle of his back. Francis Bluegill was a full-blooded Indian and I thought that made him the coolest guy in the world. He could do wolf calls that sounded like real wolves and he always said things like, "My people . . . ," "These are my people . . . ," or "My people have been . . ." Francis looked tough and serious but he laughed easy and had a voice that was soft and full and as smooth as his skin. And his face was the kind of face that didn't look like the kind of face anyone else had.

Every time my mom would see me talking to Francis she would get mad at me and say, "How often do I have to warn you about that Bluegill? He's in trouble with the law half the time. Why, his own parents are scared to death of him." This was a thing my mom often said to convey how really bad a person was. She seemed to believe the parents of these kids were being held captive and forced to cook balanced dinners, wash clothes, do their own lawn work and buy cars for their ungrateful, gun-wielding captors to drive.

When I knew I wasn't going to get caught I'd ask Francis for a ride to the Dairy Queen. He'd buy me ice cream and we'd sit in his car and clown around or talk until he'd tell me he had to get going. One day I asked him if he had a girlfriend.

"You're my girlfriend, Willbe."

I wanted to believe him but I knew he was teasing me, so I asked him again. "But for real, do you have one?"

"One? No, I do not have even one of these girlfriends."

"How come?"

"This town is too much trouble for that."

"What d'ya mean?"

"I had a girlfriend. We loved each other but I loved her more than she loved me. Her big daddy told her to never see me again and she did what he told her."

"I would never do that. Won't she even sneak out to see you?" I couldn't imagine someone wouldn't want to be with Francis.

"No. She's afraid her allowance will get cut off. Her allowance is very important to her."

I believed I was the only person Francis knew who he

told his true feelings to. To me this tied us more closely together than fifty thousand drive-in dates.

When Francis was working on his car he was usually in a kidding-around mood. While I'd hand him his tools he'd say things to me like "There are only two positions in life as far as I'm concerned. Under a car or on top of a girl."

I'd laugh and he'd say, "Hmm, hmm, hmmm. You better go on home now, I'm startin' to forget how young you are. Makes a dude hungry, being around something so fresh." Then he'd make growling sounds and act like he was going to bite me. Every time I'd leave from talking to Francis I'd feel like we had just had sex. I wasn't sure what sex felt like then but I didn't see how it could be any better than listening to Francis.

A courthouse stood in the center of the town square of Galena—the town my dad was from. Galena was twice as big as Thelma but tiny compared to Springfield. It was a wild town with more bars and liquor stores than any other type of business. There was a lot of outdoor activity there, people hung out around the square and it seemed like everyone was going or coming from somewhere— mostly the river, a bar or a rodeo.

When my family would drive down to Galena to visit relatives the first thing me and my cousin Celia would do was sneak over to the courthouse. The courthouse was where all the criminals from Stone County were held.

Thick, heavy mesh covered the windows so that the prisoners could see out but no one could see in. A big sign was posted under the window. In scary, blood-red letters was written: DO NOT TALK TO PRISONERS. Me and Celia would ignore the sign and stand out on the lawn talking to the locked-up men. They would tell us jokes or ask us questions about school or the games we played, or what boys we liked. When we would ask them why they were in jail they'd tell us they were bank robbers or murderers or cannibals who only ate young girls. But my granny, whose job it was to take food to the prisoners, told us they were really only wife beaters or disorderly drunks.

Me and Celia liked it best when the prisoners would say nasty things to us. They'd say things like "Yum, yum. I bet your little pink things taste just like sugar candy." Sometimes they would ask us to pull our panties down or they would describe what they were doing to themselves while they talked to us. We would stand there giggling and all excited until we'd be run off by the sheriff's secretary or his deputy. When the deputy would catch us he'd grab our arms and squeeze them until we yelled out in pain. He'd say, "You should be ashamed of yourselves for listening to smut. It will turn you into smut."

The deputy always looked like he had just been scrubbed down and perfectly pressed. His body was like a broomstick, not skinny, but straight and unbending.

He never laughed and he barely smiled. Everyone in Galena called him Deputy Dullwright.

When the prisoners were talking to me and Celia we would try and imagine from their voices what they looked like. To me they looked like the boys that worked in gas stations—oil-stained hands, slick, stringy hair and handsome, rare-type faces. I still don't know if the boys I liked looked the way I imagined the prisoners to look or if I imagined the prisoners to look like the kind of boys I liked.

One day my grandparents were visiting our house. It was eleven in the morning and my mom and grandmother were cooking a big lunch, the kind we always had when my grandparents visited. The doorbell rang and I ran to answer the door. A teenage girl was standing there and in a voice that sounded like she was drunk she asked if my mother was home. When my mom came to the door the girl said, "I don't know where I am."

My mom looked puzzled as she stepped down onto the porch and holding the door open with her body she looked around to see if the girl was alone.

"Where are you from?" my mom asked.

"I don't know," the girl said, starting to cry.

My mom put her arm around the girl to help her into our living room and sit her down in the rocking chair.

"What's your name?" my mom asked, like she was talking to a three-year-old.

"Bernadette."

"Well where do you live, Bernadette?"

"With my mother."

"Where's your mother live?"

The girl looked at my mom like she had just heard the announcement of a pop quiz in a chemistry class. "Boys took me away," she forced out in a loud, uncertain voice.

My mom was stunned. I walked into the hallway where my grandmother was standing. "Who is it?" she asked.

"Some girl. I think there's something wrong with her."

As my grandmother walked into the living room I heard my mom say, "You wait here with her, Mom. I'm going to call the police."

I listened to my mom on the phone as she gave the police our address. As my mom made tea for the girl she said to my grandmother, "I wonder why she picked our house to come up to? There's lots of other houses around."

"We were probably the only people home," my grandmother said matter-of-factly.

"Mom," my mom said impatiently, "I'm sure we aren't the only people at home on a Saturday morning."

"Maybe our house looks like her house," I suggested. I always got caught up in my mom's sense of intrigue. My mom liked to believe there were hidden reasons for all things people did.

"Maybe. Though I'm sure it's something not quite so simple. I think she might have amnesia. She's been through an awful ordeal," my mom added thoughtfully.

After the police came one of them walked the girl out to the car while the other policeman talked to my mom.

"You've been real helpful, ma'am. This girl's mother's been worried sick. Neither one of them though are quite right in the head. We've had a missing persons on this Bernadette for three days. Apparently this has happened to her before. Course, I think the girl may be too retarded to even know what's going on. And these boys she was with, they're always getting pulled in for something. We suspect that Francis Bluegill is the leader. She mentioned his name several times. Just goes to show you what happens when you fall in with the wrong crowd."

"You hear that, Misty? He lives right down the street here. I try to tell her he's no good."

"Listen to your mama, honey. He's trouble, has no respect for the law at all."

"Are you going to pick him up?" my mom asked.

"Well we can't do anything until we can get a more coherent statement from the girl. But I wouldn't advise talking to the Bluegills until this whole mess is cleared up." The policeman shook my mom's hand, then said, "Thanks again," and left.

As we walked onto the porch my mom said, "She came to this house to help me warn you, Misty. You see the way things happen? That poor girl probably thought she was just going to have fun. I hope I never have to tell you again to stay away from Francis and anyone like him.

If he could do that to an idiot girl, you wouldn't even want to imagine what he could do to you."

On the news that night was a report that Francis Blue-gill and six other boys, whose names had not yet been released, had taken Bernadette Hastings to Coursin's Cave and kept her there for three days while they drank liquor and had wild parties. They made her stay undressed for the whole three days and all the boys had raped her and beat her up. They said on TV that Bernadette was severely retarded and that the police were still looking for Francis Bluegill or any information as to his where-abouts. I didn't believe Francis had done what he was accused of because he had once told me he didn't like to be in crowds.

My mom was not the kind of mom to rub things in your face and make you feel crummy but it was just as bad when she said, "I'm sorry, Misty. I never thought he was that bad."

For a long time no one in our neighborhood saw any of the Bluegills. There were no cars in their drive, their shades were pulled and their doors and windows were kept shut.

Three weeks later my grandparents came back to town for a doctor appointment. While I was waiting in the doctor's office with my mom, I flipped through a News-week. I stopped on a page that had pictures of four guys with long hair and headbands, and one of the guys pic-tured was Francis Bluegill. There was a story telling how

Francis and three other men were in jail in North Dakota for holding Indian land that a big corporation wanted to use to build a paper-cup factory on. The corporation won and was going to build the factory.

Francis came back to town a few months later after he got out of jail to help his parents pack and move. His parents had gotten a famous out-of-town lawyer to sue the city and the TV stations for saying Francis was a rapist, when he wasn't even in the state. To keep from going to court they had been paid a lot of money and Francis told me they were going back to the reservation in Oklahoma where they had lived before moving to Springfield. Francis said they would be the richest Indians on the reservation and would be able to help take care of all his brothers and sisters—by that Francis meant anyone who was an Indian.

Since Francis was leaving I didn't feel like I had anything to lose by telling him I loved him. He said he would have asked me to marry him but he had pledged himself to only marry one of his people because they were a dying breed with thinning blood. Francis said the Bluegill blood was still pure and strong and that it was his duty to not let it fall just anywhere. When I told my mom what Francis had said to me she said, "I feel ashamed of myself for listening to gossip. And I never really did think his parents were afraid of him." When she said that, I knew I loved my mom for a reason and not only because she was my mom. But it made me sad to think that I didn't know that very often.

Francis became kind of a celebrity in our town for being a famous Indian fighter. Everyone, especially on our block, wanted to pretend they weren't the ones who believed Francis was a rapist. I would read about Francis sometimes in the newspaper or talk to his good friend Bobby Brown. They still wrote and sometimes Bobby even visited him in Oklahoma. One day Bobby told me that he had just come back from a wedding, Francis's wedding. He said it had been a big church wedding and that the bride was the daughter of a rich Oklahoma oil tycoon. He said she had long blond hair and sea-blue eyes and that she was more beautiful than Marilyn Monroe and Mia Farrow put together. Bobby said the two of them were so much in love that they just kissed or stared at each other.

I cried and because I wanted to hate Francis I told my mom what had happened. She was always encouraging me to hate guys and realize they'll do you wrong. But my mom said, "Love makes people do things they might think they could never do. And love is as important and noble as anything in the world. True love is a real cause because it's a real cure. If all the bad people in the world found love they wouldn't be bad anymore and if all the greedy people found love they wouldn't be greedy anymore and if all the sad people found it they wouldn't be sad. You should be happy for him, Misty. It's a rare thing for people to fall in love. And it was something that was obviously meant to be."

I felt sick. I wondered what that meant. It didn't seem fair to have to love somebody who was only meant to love somebody else. It didn't seem fair that unless something was meant to be it wasn't ever going to happen or unhappen for you no matter what you did. But mostly it didn't seem fair that you only found out what was meant to be after it already was.

It was weird to hear my mom talking that way about love and I wondered if she was having an affair. Usually she said terrible things about people in love. She believed people in love were the same as people who were in caged-up wings of dilapidating hospitals that lay on the outskirts of towns, and she'd say, "Neither one of them has a notion of what is happening in the real world. They need to be locked away to keep from hurting themselves while under the influences of drugs, visions or romance."

She believed that women who fell in love were assigned to a life of hand-washing dishes, hanging out laundry and scrubbing up dirty floors and bathrooms after lots of whining children. My mom was convinced that only women who were clever and cold enough to marry for money or become a mistress to a millionaire would ever be really happy. When I would ask my mom why it seemed like she was trying to keep me from falling in love she'd answer, "To spare you. Because life is about promise, Misty. But love, that's only about broken promises. Broken promises and broken hearts."

I didn't ever listen to her, though, because like all other kids I knew my life would never be like hers.

——————

THERE WERE A LOT of tornado alerts in Springfield. Tornado alerts and crime caused the same kind of reaction in my town. When one or the other had happened it would be on the front page of the newspaper, special bulletins would flash across the TV screen, and everyone would get scared and excited. A tornado had never actually hit Springfield and no one had ever been murdered brutally. But everyone was always waiting for the day one of them would happen.

On school days when there were tornado watches it felt like the last day of school. We didn't have to do any schoolwork, the teachers didn't yell at us and all the kids giggled and told stories about relatives or friends who had been sucked up in cyclones or seen pigs and cows being lifted up and away into the sky. Sometimes you would hear how the person had seen the animal be dropped back down but usually nobody knew where the thing ended up.

Tornadoes and criminals were like the Pied Piper to us. The mystery of a tornado could entice you to stand outside and watch it. Kidnappers and child molesters might try to lure you with candy or money or car rides. If you followed either of them, though, you'd be like all the poor children of Hamelin—taken away and trapped, never to see your parents or your pets or the world as you knew it again. But then, the Pied Piper promised a lot more to us than parents did.

The criminals in Springfield were always given a nickname depending on what crime they had committed. The Candy Man put arsenic on children's lollipops. The Catfish took police four months to catch. He stalked around homes waiting for the husbands to leave and the kids to be put to bed. Then, with his naked body covered in mud, he would sneak in and expose himself to the startled housewife.

The Swinger, like most other villains in Springfield, was never caught. He crashed cocktail parties that rich people had and would force a woman into the bathroom and make her shower in front of him, then leave with her clothes. He was especially famous because all the victims had described him as "extremely handsome, he looked just like Gregory Peck."

One Halloween a man who'd been dubbed The Doctor was said to be still on the prowl. He was called The Doctor because he used ether to knock out his victims before he robbed them. Everyone on the south side was in a state of panic. People were installing security systems and putting their valuables in safety deposit boxes and storage lockers.

The day before Halloween, school issued letters to all the parents that said, "So far The Doctor has only stolen money, appliances and jewelry. But as we all know nothing is more valuable than our children. Since we can't know how the deviant mind works we suggest that parents make this an early Halloween. Have your children in by 9:00 P.M."

We had to bring back the letters with our parents' signatures or we wouldn't be allowed to leave school on Halloween until a parent had been contacted.

Me and Toni Bartlett had planned to go trick-or-treating that year together but decided that since we would be in costume it would be a perfect time to capture The Doctor instead. We had decided he was holed up in Kings Way Methodist Church. The church had caught on fire a few weeks earlier and been closed down for repair. Me and Toni believed no one would think to look inside a church for a crook and were convinced the crook would know the same thing. We were proud of ourselves for being able to think like the criminal mind.

After school we went to my house and got dressed in our outfits. Toni was a gypsy and I was a hobo. My mom took pictures of us and kept telling us to be extra careful.

Me and Toni were best friends that year. She had transferred to our school from the north side. We first met at Kings Way. Even though my parents still didn't believe in church I had started going to Sunday school. I started because so many of the kids at school went and I thought being in the choir and going on special field trips and having Bible classes sounded like fun. I would go to Sunday school, to choir practice on Tuesdays and Bible study on Wednesday nights. Bible study wasn't so much about reading the Bible as it was about studying the difference between right and wrong. Still every once in a while the teacher would talk about Jesus.

One Thursday night we had a special guest speaker who was invited to tell us about her experience of being saved, which had happened to her several weeks earlier. We were motioned to sit around the lady as she witnessed to us. Most of the kids, especially the boys, passed notes back and forth or pinched or tickled or teased each other. Normally I did the same stuff but as soon as this woman started talking I ignored the other kids. The lady had a whispery voice and her hair was soft and white like the hair I had seen on pictures of angels. She said, "I had hit rock bottom. I was in a personal crisis in my own life. My husband and I were fighting and I had started to drink and I had abandoned my faith. When that happens your whole life crumbles.

"One night I was alone and I was laying in bed, crying. The room was dark. I started to pray to the Lord to hear my prayers and suddenly the room filled with a white light. I knew it was Jesus. As he entered my body it felt airless, weightless, my tears were gone. And for the first time in months a smile came to my face. I felt free. I had been saved.

"Since that time my life has been very different. I'm no longer sad. I know the Lord is with me and I don't feel scared anymore."

When she got done talking the teacher asked if we had any questions but no one raised their hands. I wanted to ask her why she looked so sad if she felt so good but I was too embarrassed to let the other kids know I had been listening.

After the class that night me and Toni and Mickey Beechum and John Sinclair snuck into the cathedral part of the church. It had just been built and was scheduled to hold its first service the next Sunday. I had a crush on Mickey, who was two years older than me. Toni and John were going steady.

The new cathedral had big stained-glass windows and slate floors. It was an A-frame and had the highest ceiling of any building I had ever been in. As soon as we got inside Toni and John snuck away together and me and Mickey explored. We went up into the organ chamber and the choir section. We played on the pulpit and ran through all the pews. Then we went and sat behind the altar. Mickey had cigarettes and he asked if I wanted one.

"Do you think we'll go to hell if we smoke in church?" I asked, trying to make it sound like a joke.

"This isn't a church yet if the reverend hasn't talked in it," Mickey said. Then he lit us two cigarettes. I looked at the stained glass. The parking-lot lights were shining through them and you could see Jesus and angels and crosses and people hanging on crosses in the tinted light.

"Did you listen to that lady tonight?" I asked Mickey.

"Naw. Buzz was stabbing me every seventeen seconds with his new army knife."

"Did he hurt you?"

"You kidding?" he answered, looking at me like I was weird.

I blushed and said, "I can forge Mrs. Krebs' name on hall passes," hoping that would make up for asking such a stupid question.

"No kidding?"

"I have a book of hall passes I stole."

"You probably shouldn't say that in here, Misty. You know how God is about stealing. I think forgery is a sin too."

I felt my face turn red. It seemed like no matter what I did, boys always thought I was stupid. I knew if Toni had told him the same thing I'd just said he would have fallen in love with her. But me saying it had only made him think I was more dumb.

"Hey, I'm teasing you," Mickey said as he put his arm around me, then moved onto his knees to face me. "You can say or do whatever you want here. Look." Then Mickey started kissing me. It was the first time a boy ever put his tongue in my mouth. Then he put his hand up under my shirt. I was still completely flat but he slipped his hand up under my bra and kept his hand there while he French-kissed me. I didn't know if I was feeling so scared because I wondered if Mickey would like the way I kissed or because I had never gone that far before or because I was afraid I was going to burn in hell.

The next day Toni told me that her and John had watched us making out. She said John had tried to get her to do the same thing but she had refused. I felt bad that Toni and John had seen us and I figured I was a worse person than Toni was, especially since her and John went steady together until she moved away the next year and Mickey had never talked to me again after that night.

Before me and Toni had gone out trick-or-treating we wrote a note to place in the Meads' mailbox. They never unlocked their gates on Halloween and no matter how many kids would try it was impossible to get to their front door to ring the bell.

The Meads lived three streets over from my parents' house. Their house looked like a castle. It had four towers and windows with diamond-shaped lead panes that made the glass look like it was glistening all the time. Moss and ivy grew up one side of the house, which was shaded by gigantic pine trees. Even though you couldn't see the swimming pool we knew it was there because you could see two high-diving boards. They had a yard that was as big as our whole school ground. It was enclosed by a fence that looked like hundreds of tall iron spears stuck into the ground. Their drive was a long dirt road with ornate iron gates that were always kept locked, and it led to a garage that was bigger than any house in the neighborhood. I had always wished that we could live in the Meads' house. In a place that big I believed I could run away and never be found without even having to leave home.

No one in our neighborhood knew the Meads personally. All we knew was that they had seven cars that were foreign and hired help that wore uniforms. Every time we would drive by the Meads' house my mom would say, "What I wouldn't give to see the inside of that place."

My dad said Mr. Mead was in the Mafia. He believed the only way anyone ever got rich was through crime and he'd always say, "If you meet anyone who has a lot of money you better watch your back while you're checking their money for bloodstains."

My mom and dad would go into the same fight every time we passed the Meads' house together.

"You just believe all rich people are bad because you don't have any money," she would accuse my dad.

"I've got all the money I need," my dad would respond.

"You need. Sure, you've got enough to buy your boats and guns and cars. What about what I want?"

"What do you want? Diamonds, furs, fancy clothes? Those things are just a waste. What can you do with 'em? Nothing."

"I'd like a nice house," my mom would say.

"We've got one. You just don't need more than we've got. You buy yourself whatever you want anyway."

"Cheap, dimestore stuff. My clothes are all basement bargains. I have to go without so at least the girls don't suffer."

It was true that my mom would buy me and Angie our clothes from the nicest stores in town. She would spend less money on a dress for herself than she would on a nightgown for us. Except that my mom never bought us just nightgowns, they were always peignoir sets.

I loved all my clothes even though my mom claimed she couldn't satisfy me.

My dad didn't happen to see the value in the same things me and Angie and my mom liked. He'd tell us he figured that was because we were girls and would say, "I guess females just have a need for useless items."

And my mom would always answer him, "Well I guess my being with you proves your point."

Sometimes my dad would laugh at this and sometimes he would get really mad. But always he would answer, "You should've married some goddamn mobster. I'd like to see how happy you'd be then."

Me and Toni had decided the Meads were going to be the next victims of The Doctor, and in our note we told them that we were going to the abandoned church to capture The Doctor and save the Meads from being robbed. We signed our names and left our address in case they wanted to mail us a reward.

When we got to the church we tried to figure out how

we were going to get in but when we tried the front door it was open so we walked in. The church was dark, but there was a glow like nighttime outside. Toni whispered, "He must be in here because he forgot to lock the door."

"What are we going to do when we catch him?"

"We'll sneak up behind him. He'll probably be counting his money so he'll be busy. We'll sneak up and throw our trick-or-treat bags over his head and then we'll suffocate him."

"That's a good idea."

We tiptoed all through the church. Every creak we made or breath we took we believed was the sound of The Doctor.

As we walked into the coat room we looked down and saw a door cut into the floor.

"A trap door," I said breathlessly.

"That must be where he is," Toni whispered back.

"We have to be really quiet now. I don't know if we can lift this up."

As me and Toni were on our knees trying to slip our fingers into the crevices of the door we heard the sound of heavy footsteps close to where we were.

"Omigod. It's him," Toni whispered hysterically.

"What're we going to do?"

We crouched lower on our knees thinking that might hide us.

"Quick. We have to get the door up. We'll hide here," she said, trying to keep her voice down.

74

"We can't go down there. He'll still kill us but no one will ever find our bodies."

As we were trying to unstick our fingers from the door we saw two big feet between our hands. I started praying to God to please not let us be murdered. But I didn't really think he would listen since I had made out with Mickey Beechum in his church. Just then I felt a man's hand grab my shirt collar. Toni was starting to cry and I began to plead with the man to spare us as he lifted me up to my feet.

"Spare you, my ass."

I didn't know if I felt more fear or relief to recognize the angry voice.

"I've been looking all over the place for you two," my dad yelled. "Get your tails out to the car now! You know what time it is?"

Toni was crying but I couldn't move. My dad pulled me by my collar out to the car.

"What the hell were you up to? If I'd been the police you'd be in jail right now for trespassing or vandalism. What did you do? Break in here?" my dad demanded.

"It was unlocked. We were looking for the robber," I said. I was so afraid that my voice and body had gone completely helpless.

"What robber?"

"The Doctor," I said. "We thought he was hiding out here."

"By the time we get home you're going to wish to hell that I was The Doctor instead of your dad!"

Toni was sobbing and begging my dad not to tell her parents. But I already knew he wasn't going to tell on her. As mad as my parents would get at me, they went out of their way to protect other kids from getting in trouble with their parents. I could never understand why they didn't care if me and Angie got in trouble as much as they didn't want my friends to.

When we got home my mom was making hot chocolate. She tried to calm my dad down. When one of them was mad at us the other one usually tried to get the other one from being so upset.

My mom was in a really good mood that night because the Meads had called her after they had read the note me and Toni had left in their mailbox and asked my mom to come over to their house. They didn't want to tell her the story on the phone because they thought she would be too worried. My mom said the Meads were a really old couple and even though she had only gotten to stand in their hallway she said she saw a wide, circular marble staircase and huge crystal chandelier that looked exactly the way she had imagined their house to look. She said their butler had brought the note into her on a silver tray and that the old woman was wearing a long, maroon velvet dress and the man had on a gray silk smoking jacket. My mom said she felt as if she had just walked into a movie.

My dad was even madder at me because my mom said she had completely disproven my dad's theory about all people with money. She said the Meads were so old and nice they couldn't have done anything awful to get so rich.

––––––––––––––
––––––––

BEFORE I BECAME completely devoted to my own life I spent a lot of time with my dad. We'd hang out on the lakes, in fields or woods or drive on back roads looking for new hunting spots. On our drives I would see lots of dead animals laying by the side of the road. Sometimes they would look like they were sleeping but usually they would be busted open—veins and eyeballs popped out. If it was fresh the blood and entrails would glisten moist, almost reflect the sunlight.

My dad liked to have me go along with him but most of the time he didn't want me to talk. When we were on the lake he'd tell me to listen to the water slapping against the boat and in the woods he would tell me to listen to the trees rustling or for the sounds of animals scampering through the fallen leaves. One morning we were sitting way out in the woods under a tall tree. My dad had his gun laying next to him. We were waiting for squirrel. It was fall and the air was clean and cold. It was a dark, cloudy morning, the kind my dad said were best for squirrel hunting. That morning my dad was in a really good mood. My mom had made us a big breakfast before we left and they had kissed each other bye. I sat under the tree and listened to all the sounds that get carried in the open air. After a while I whispered, "I could live out here."

"Me too," my dad whispered back. I looked at my dad, leaning against the tree, his knees pulled into his chest, a blade of grass dangling from his mouth. I had said I could live in the woods because I was happy right then, but as soon as I got hungry or cold or wanted to go to the bathroom I would want to be home. My dad really could have, really wanted to live in the woods forever.

I knew some things about my dad and his life. I knew he didn't like being asked for or told things. I knew he hated policemen, salesmen, game wardens and highway patrolmen. I knew his dad had left his mom after their tenth kid was born and moved up the road to live with another woman. My dad would tell me, "The ol' man would come around to beat the hell out of us every now and then, but he'd apologize for it later, saying he guessed he just needed to hurt something. Then he'd take me hunting or fishing to make up for it. I guess it was hard on him too, having so many kids he couldn't take care of."

I knew my dad had worked since he was six years old and had left home when he was twelve to do harvest work in California. He had been a pilot in the air force and moved back to Galena when he got out, then he met my mom, then he started working as a fireman.

As we sat under the tree I whispered to my dad, "Dad, did you always want to be a fireman?"

"Never wanted to be anything, I guess," he said, as he opened his Thermos to pour himself coffee. "I just liked the hours at the fire department. If you gotta have a job might as well have one that you don't have to work at. If I didn't have you kids I wouldn't work at all."

"Do you wish you didn't have to work?" I asked.

"Oh, sure I do."

"Mom hates working too," I said, closing the Thermos back for my dad.

He laughed. "She hates everything."

"No, she doesn't."

"No, she's a good ol' girl really," my dad said as he patted my thigh.

"Do you guys love each other?" I asked. I was always asking my parents that and every time I did they acted like I had never asked it before.

"We're together," my dad answered.

"Why'd you ask Mom to marry you?"

"People don't hardly ever know why they did something they did that long ago. Maybe they don't even know the minute after they do it." My dad stared up into the high branches of the trees as he spoke. If he heard a bough shake or crack, his eyes would dart to that direction to see what was there.

"How come you guys are always fighting?"

"We're not always fighting. I wish you'd quit saying such crazy things all the time."

"How come you fight when you do?"

"Got something to be mad about, I figure."

"Would you be upset if Mom left?" I asked.

"Not if she thought that would make her happy," he answered.

"What if she died?"

"What the hell kind of question is that?"

"She could die. Lots of people do," I said.

"Well she's not going to die," my dad said firmly.

"How do you know?"

"Well we all die sometime. It's just something you can't stop to think about is all." My dad wasn't whispering anymore and he was looking down at me with a smile.

"What do you do when someone you love dies?" I asked, thinking of all the dead people I had heard about.

"Well you just go on. You don't have any choice."

"I wouldn't be able to go on if something happened to you or Mom or Angie," I said, feeling tears come up in my eyes.

"Well you'd just have to, sis. You'd be real sad for a while but then it would get OK."

"Dad, do you really believe hell is being alive in a coffin for eternity?" I'd heard my dad tell people this was what he believed hell was. It made me really scared for my dad because I knew how much he would suffer to be in a jet-black place and not be able to move his body or hear any sounds.

"I guess I do. I can't think of anything that would be more hellish," he said sadly.

"How do you go to hell?"

"Well you have to kill a person for no reason."

I was so relieved because I knew then that even if I did the worst thing in the world, which would be to kill someone, I would only do it for a good reason. I decided to believe my dad and never listen to another person who told me you could go to hell for lying or cheating or fighting or having sex more often than you had kids.

"So you don't believe Granpa went to hell?" I asked just to be sure.

"Naw, he was too mean to go to hell. Only some pretty angels could tame him." My dad laughed.

"When did Granpa die?" I asked.

"When you were little. I guess you were six or seven."

"Were you sad?"

"His dogs were. Course, he was better to his dogs than he was to us. They gave the death howl for five nights. He had ten bird dogs and it was a mournful thing to hear but everyone in town got irritated after the first two nights. If I hadn't been able to get some money out of those dogs I would've shot them myself the first night."

Around dusk time as we were driving home I saw a big dog walking along the side of the highway, using its teeth to drag a larger dog by the neck. The dog being pulled through the gravel was dead and stiff—so stiff it looked like a poster of a dog.

The dog walked along the side of the highway like there was nothing else in the world except the path he was on. I asked my dad why the dog was carrying the dead dog.

"It's his mate probably. He's taking her home to bury her. Dogs do that too. Only difference is he won't ever get over her. Dogs are the most faithful creatures on earth."

My dad, like his dad, had lots of hunting dogs. My mom always complained that he treated them better than he did her. My dad's favorite dog was one he'd had since she was a puppy. Her name was Sally. He would get drunk with her and feed her special foods my mom had cooked and let her ride in the front seat of his truck with him.

Sally won lots of hunting trophies and men were always offering my dad thousands of dollars for her, but there wasn't a thing in the world he would have taken. Once he bred Sally to another prize-winning pointer. While she was pregnant my dad made all kinds of fancy foods for her, he put extra hay in her doghouse and as it got colder put a heat lamp in her house to keep her warm.

After the puppies were born my dad acted like he was the father. It had been snowing, so my dad put another heat lamp in the doghouse to keep the puppies protected. One night I woke up in the middle of the night. I looked out my bedroom window and saw flames where the doghouses were supposed to be. My mom and dad were running with blankets and buckets of water. Then I fell back to sleep because I thought I was dreaming. The next morning it was really quiet in our house and my mom made me and Angie whisper. She told us that the dog-houses had caught on fire and that all of Sally's pups were dead. She said my dad got Sally out and had to tie ropes around her feet to keep her from trying to run back in the burning house after her puppies. My dad was really depressed and for days he blamed himself for the heat lamps. Sally walked with her head hung low and tail drooped and my dad said she would never be the same dog again.

Six months later my dad took Sally out in the woods and shot her in the head. He said she wasn't able to hunt anymore and wasn't worth the food he had to waste on her.

When I would go fishing with my dad we would stop at some roadside tavern on the way home. When we'd go hunting we would stop in a beer joint that was off in the woods. When we'd drive to Galena we'd end up spending the evening in a local bar. It was OK for me if other kids were around because we'd get money thrown at us for the jukebox or pinball or potato chips—anything to keep us out of the way. But that was rare. Most of my time in these places was spent being entertained by the men who were too drunk or lame to play pool or by the ladies in the bar. They looked the same in every joint we ended up in—big dyed hair, tight stretch pants the color of bike reflectors, big boobs, and soft, white, fleshy arms popping out of sleeveless, low-cut jersey tops. They all had names like Gloria, Delores or Maxine.

These women would pay me a lot of attention. They'd make sure the bartendar put straws, cherries, oranges and grenadine in my Cokes, ask me what song I wanted them to punch in on the jukebox, and sometimes even give me things to keep—like an old compact with only a little rouge left around the gold rim inside or lipstick that was some bright, awful color, flattened out and hard in the tube. Still, I never liked these women much. They asked too many questions—"Where's your mama?" "How old's your sister?" "Does your mama know you're here?" "What's your mama do when you and your daddy are out on the town?" "Is your mama pretty?"—and acted too familiar, calling me "sugar" and "angel," and calling my dad "baby" or "honey" or "you devil."

Sometimes my mom and Angie would be with me when my dad stopped at a bar. Then he'd make us all wait out in the car until he was through in the bar, which could be three or four in the morning. If it was winter we'd have to keep turning the heater on even though it didn't warm us up, because my mom would roll the windows down so we wouldn't fall asleep and die of gas fumes. As awful as it could get waiting in the car for my dad, watching the door to the beer joint every time it opened, hoping it would be him, it was not awful to be in a close place with my mom and Angie. We never fought those nights, no matter how cold or tired we got. My mom would sing songs or play games. She had one game where she would hide a piece of gum in her mouth for us to find. Me and Angie would be on either side of my mom, pulling her lips apart and out and rubbing our fingers around her teeth, trying to push each other's hands away. My mom would act like she was choking and stammer, "You're br-breaking my neck." By the time we'd give up looking for the gum, we'd all be breathless and gasping. We'd beg my mom to show us where she hid her gum. "Someday, when you've got you own kids, I'll show you." I'd ask, "But what if we die before that?" And my mom would laugh.

My mom was really beautiful when she laughed. Her eyes glistened and her head would fall back. She laughed a lot with me and Angie and sometimes around friends. When she laughed around my dad he'd call her crazy or drunk and give her a look like she was weird. When my dad put my mom down this way she'd get upset and start to cry. The more worked up she'd become the more closed off he'd get, which would make her more worked up until she was screaming at him, "Why don't you go somewhere you'll be happier?" "Why do you stay here then?" "Why don't you find someone who isn't crazy?" He'd just glare at her and say, "You're nuts."

When you're a kid you have a tendency to take to, to believe the voice that is most definite and calm because that's where you think you're safer. Grown-ups talk about how smart children are in these ways. They say it's because children decide things from their instincts and if a child takes to you that proves you're a good person. But that's not really true. The first time I saw a bumblebee buzzing on a dandelion it looked soft and playful. It stung my finger as soon as I tried to pet it. My instincts about bees were different after that experience. I think my only true instinct, one that didn't come from something learned, was to beware of things that were bigger than me until it proved it wasn't going to eat me.

After the first three hours of waiting in the car we would have run through all the car-seat games and songs we knew. Then we'd just talk and I'd always get the conversation to the point where I'd ask my mom to tell us the story of how her and my dad got together. She'd say, "Oh, I don't feel like telling that story again." But me and Angie would plead with her until she gave in. She'd lean back against the car door and sigh in a way to make it obvious how much she didn't want to do this, then she'd begin, the same way each time, "I was on my way to Ava with Pat Vernon and her brother Henry, who I was in love with. I always hoped that Henry would ask me out but he never did. The Vernons were rich. It was OK for Pat to be my girlfriend but her folks would've never allowed Henry to go out with me. He was dating Marcia Beardsley, they were the most popular couple in our school, they were in our yearbook as that. Everyone thought they were perfect together. The Beardsleys were a big name around and the Vernons did everything they could to be sure Henry would hang on to Marcia.

"But this weekend Marcia was away—her daddy had paid for her to go to Kansas City to get a new wardrobe— and I was going to be able to dance with Henry all night long.

"I was wearing that yellow dress, embossed with the waterfall scenes. Henry kept saying, 'You're a star, Phaera. The most beautiful woman these hills ever produced.' "

By the time my mom got to this part her voice would be airier and her words would drift more together, she'd be staring way off out the window, beyond the gravel lot we were parked in, beyond the highway. And it would feel like me and Angie weren't even there anymore.

"When we got to the dance I noticed your dad in the parking lot. Pat said, 'That's Will Groves.' Everyone knew the Groveses by name, they were the wildest bunch around. I'd never seen Will before but had heard plenty. Pat had a bit of a crush on him herself even though she already had plans to marry Vic. But all the girls had a crush on your dad. A fact he never failed to take advantage of.

"As we crossed the parking lot I looked over at your dad. He was sitting on the hood of his orange Chevrolet convertible, four or five other kids were standing around him, and he looked over and stared straight through me. I felt self-conscious. Pat said, 'He likes you, look at that.'

"Inside the dance hall I danced with Henry. I still was in love with him but I couldn't get out of my head the way your dad had looked at me. I should have walked home at that moment but I didn't. After I had danced a few dances with Henry your dad came over and said, 'You look all steamed up. Why don't you cool off? I'll take you for a little drive.' I turned him down. I wasn't about to get off public property with him. So he said, 'Well let's just sit in my car. C'mon, it's hot in here, you could faint and I might not be close enough to catch you.' "

Here my mom would interrupt the story to look me straight in the eye and tell me to never, ever listen to a man with a smooth line, and how charmers were the worst men on earth and that there was never an exception to that rule. Before she would go on with the story I'd have to assure her I'd steer clear of charming guys but I knew if someone offered to catch me if I fainted I most definitely would fall in love with them.

My mom would still be sounding mad when she returned to where she left off. "So I went out and sat in his car with him. I felt so excited walking across the lot to his car. At the time I took it for attraction, though I'm pretty sure now it was a feeling that's not too different than people feel on their walk to the gas chamber.

"Your dad's car was the most beautiful orange I'd ever seen and he kept it spotless. Every girl that walked by said, 'Hi, Willy.' But your dad was clever. He treated me like I was the only girl alive. Clever, handsome, smart, funny, that was Will Groves. He could've been a movie star, a pilot, a doctor. He could've been anything he wanted but he never wanted to get out of these hills, moving sixty miles to Springfield was too big a move for him. Had I known then what I know now, but I didn't.

"We sat out in his car the rest of the night and talked.

I remember I was surprised that he was so sincere. Back then your dad cared about what I said. He listened to me that night like I was saying the most important things in the world. I told him how embarrassed I was my parents had named me Phaera and that he was the first person who didn't go, 'Huh? Pharaoh?' when I told him my name. Your dad told me he liked my name, that it was a name you couldn't forget. And he said it fit me because it was feminine and mysterious.

"Will told me things about himself. He told me that when he was ten he had been at one of his sisters' bedside when she died. He was holding her hand.

"We laughed too that night. When Pat came out of the dance hall to get me, your dad asked me to go out with him the next weekend. When he came to pick me up that Saturday Mom and Dad fell head over heels for him. As we were driving to Hollister to go to a county fair, he told me he hadn't been able to think about anything all week except me. He said he believed if he traveled all over the world he'd never find a girl he'd rather spend time with. And one month later we were married. Just too silly kids too young to know any better."

My mom still had the yellow dress she'd worn that night, it was hanging in our basement under plastic wrap. I had seen lots of pictures of my dad's orange Chevrolet with him sitting on the hood looking the way he must've looked to my mom. But I had never seen my mom and dad talk to each other the way they had that night.

As soon as i knew what sex was I knew my mom was pregnant with me when they got married. My parents were really defensive on this subject. One time my mom slapped me when I asked her about it. And one time when she was drunk she said, "Yes, I was pregnant. Why else would I have married the sonofabitch? So now you know it's all your fault we live in this hell."

By the time my mom said this to me our family was so far gone it only felt painful to hear because I knew it should be.

I didn't think any of my friends had parents who fought the way mine did. No one knew they fought, though, because my mom and dad cared a whole lot about appearances. Most of the time they fought about my dad staying out—not coming home or calling for days at a time. My dad would say he was in the woods or on the lake and couldn't get to a phone. Me and Angie believed him but my mom knew him better than we did, I think.

I always got in the middle of my parents' fights—begging them to quit yelling, or pushing my dad away if he was getting physical with my mom. Instead of making them stop, it only made the fights louder or more violent. When I'd try to protect my mom, my dad would drag me to my room and threaten to hurt me if I came out again. I'd lay on my bed crying and shaking so hard I wouldn't be able to catch my breath. Every time I'd hear them hit or shove each other I'd want to run out of my room and throw myself between them. Angie would go straight to her room when my parents started fighting and not come out until the next day. I'd ask her how she could not care what was happening, why she didn't try and help me stop them and she'd only say, "Because I don't hear them."

Sometimes my parents would go out together on weekend nights. I would feel my stomach begin to squirm and tighten as I watched my mom dress up to go out. Usually they'd be going to some kind of party and my mom would say they'd be home by midnight. I'd want to believe her. I'd look at her in her dangling earrings and velvet high heels, her hair hanging down soft over her shoulders and wonder if this would be the last time I'd ever see her. She would look so pretty on those nights. My dad would be waiting for her to change her purse and pick out a coat and he'd whistle at her when she'd finally walk into the hallway—the signal it was time for them to go.

Then they'd walk out the door, I'd watch them back out of the drive and I'd start crying. As soon as it was midnight I'd go sit in the rocker that faced out our picture window. Our driveway was at the foot of a steep hill that forked. One road went to a dead end and the other turned into a main road. I'd watch all the car lights come down the hill hoping the next car would be my parents.

By four in the morning I would be hysterical. I'd want to call the police, the hospitals and the bars I thought they could be at. But I had learned a long time ago that if my dad found out I had done that he would cause me more pain than I could cause myself.

On those nights I'd get images of my dad killing my mom in a fight or getting in a car wreck because they were drunk and yelling at each other. I had watched so many bad fights with them and been in the car when my dad would get mad and start speeding around curves that it never felt like something I was making up in my own head at the moment.

Sometimes my mom and dad wouldn't come home for two or three days. The whole time I'd sit in the house and wait for them to call. Anytime the phone would ring I'd run to answer it, and tears would fill my eyes as soon as I heard someone's voice besides my mom's. When my mom finally would call she'd say my dad had driven them to Arkansas or Oklahoma and that they were in a hotel and she was trying to get him to leave. She'd tell me not to worry, that they'd be home soon, that she loved me and to be careful in the kitchen.

Angie was able to take advantage of these weekends to do whatever she wanted but I spent the whole time in a kind of emergency-room limbo. When Angie would finally come home from wherever she had been playing she'd try to stop me from worrying. She'd make us brownies or scrambled eggs and bacon, and on these nights she'd let me sleep in her bed with her. We'd lay in bed and talk about my parents. Angie would ask, "Why do you always do this? You know they never do what they say they're going to."

"Because I believe them when they say they'll come back. They know how worried I get. I feel like something awful must have happened to them or they wouldn't do this to us."

"They don't think about us," Angie would answer.

"How are you able to not care when they do this?"

" 'Cause there's nothing I can do about it."

"If they knew we both felt the same way maybe they'd be different."

"No, they wouldn't. Besides, I'd rather they were gone so I don't have to listen to them."

"But what if they hurt each other?"

"That won't happen."

"It could. You know how they get. Remember on *Kraft Suspense Theatre,* where the man pushed the woman and she fell and hit her head on the corner of a coffee table and it killed her?"

"Yea but I think it's harder to kill someone in real life or one of them would already be dead by now." Angie's voice would start to get weary and she'd roll over on her side. I'd lay there next to her for a minute and wish it was so easy for me to put all my thoughts away. "What would you do if they died, Angie?"

"I don't know. Let's go to sleep."

"Would you care?"

"I guess."

"Would you cry?"

"Probably. But I just don't think about it. I don't know why I don't, I just don't. You should try to go to sleep, though."

"I can't. Please stay up a little longer and talk to me."

"I'm tired."

I knew if I started talking about sex it would make Angie get a burst of energy. That was about the only thing she found entertaining at this time of the night. "Guess who I made out with the other day?" I asked, knowing that would make her roll over and look at me.

"No one," Angie said, still with her back to me.

"It was right here in the house . . . on the couch . . . in the living room."

Angie still didn't budge.

"He tried to feel me out," I said.

Angie turned over immediately. "Did you let him?" she asked, wide awake.

"Guess who it was," I said.

"Dan Miles?"

"No."

"Rick Schultz?"

"No."

"Tommy Shirley?"

"Maybe."

"Tommy Shirley? You're lying."

"Uh huh."

"Did you let him?"

"I let him put his hand up my shirt."

"Bet he was disappointed."

"Ha ha. He also tried to touch me you know where."

"Tried?"

"I didn't let him." I squealed.

"Is he a good kisser?"

"Not really. He's sort of like kissing a wall. He presses his mouth on your mouth so hard your neck feels like it's gonna break."

"Did you French?"

"Well he stuck his tongue in my mouth but he just stuck it in there and didn't do anything with it. It felt weird."

"Too bad. He's awful cute."

"I know but I don't think he's so cute anymore."

"Would you kiss him again?"

"Probably, but I wouldn't like it." I was actually glad when a guy would kiss me bad because then I knew I could never be under his power.

In the sixth grade I went to my first boy/girl party. "Hey Jude" was playing on the record player and Phillip Post, who was an eighth-grader, asked me to slow dance. He kissed me through almost the whole song. I fell so deeply in love with him that I knew even if I lived long enough to actually meet and marry one of the Beatles I would never get over Phillip.

When you're a kid love is filled with so much more longing it seems deeper. Love is always unrequited when you're that age because either the guy you want is older and only thinks of you as a baby or you love someone your same age so you're both too young to really fulfill anything.

Doug Waters was the first boyfriend I had where we said we loved each other. We were in the seventh grade. Doug was way ahead of his time. He had long hair, wore a fringed leather jacket, rode a motorcycle and never looked any adult in the face. Even though we were in the same grade I never knew how old Doug was. I only knew he had flunked some grades and that he shaved his face.

People gossiped that Doug smoked pot but that didn't bother me. I believed he was more of a right kind of person than the other kids at school. They only cared about what people thought and spread lies behind each other's back. When I told Melanie Sherwood that I thought it was OK for people to smoke pot she passed it around that I was a slut and a dope fiend. After that even high school girls would come up to me and say things like, "I think it's gross that you're a doper," or "You better care a little more what people think of you. You're getting a really bad reputation."

Even though the whole school thought I was bad news I was still invited to Jane Steinway's boy/girl birthday party. It was so big that she got to have it at her parents' country club. And there was a live band.

I invited Doug to come with me. We ended up making out most of the night on top of a pile of coats that had been thrown under the coatrack. I remember feeling self-conscious because I knew I would have hickeys on my neck later and I thought, "I guess I really am a bad person." When we finally got up there were four parents glaring at us. They looked directly at me with an expression that made me know how people who are deformed or in freak shows feel every day.

Afterwards me and Doug walked around outside. I wanted to dance and eat cake with the other kids but Doug said, "I'm not into hanging out in joints where there are chaperones. It's too uptight."

As we walked around the swimming pool I wondered why I had done what I had done. When Doug was kissing me I kept thinking about the people around us. I knew they would all be talking about me the next day. But I just couldn't make myself stop. I mean I did ask if we could get up a few times but Doug just kept on kissing me. And I was too weak from feeling the way he was making me feel to be able to argue.

Then I knew that a good kiss would always be my downfall. It made me lose my will and even who I was. I quit being afraid, I quit being mad and I quit feeling sad. I melted completely under the power of the person who could take those feelings away. I guess it proved to me that I was the kind of girl you'd read about in the newspapers. One who had robbed banks, stolen cars or gone on murder sprees with a wild guy because he had possessed her mind.

"What do you think it feels like to go all the way?" Angie asked. From this point in our conversation it was hard to say anything without giggling hysterically.

"Ugh. I don't know, that part of it seems pretty gross. I wish you only had to make out."

"I know. Remember when we saw the dogs doing it? That was disgusting. They didn't look like they were having fun at all. And when Mom and Dad do it. Yuk."

"It kills me the way they think we don't know what's going on," I said.

"I know, and I hate the way mom acts when they come out of the bedroom. All mushy and gushing, calling us 'baby' and stuff."

"She acts like she's drunk. And that smile she gets on her face makes her look like an idiot."

"And they always get into a fight after they do it."

"I saw 'em do it one time," I said. "Mom's back was to me, she was naked and sitting on Dad. He looked at me and started laughing and Mom turned her head to face me. She looked at me the way those guys on TV look, when they get caught standing over a dead body with a bloody knife in their hands, only they're really innocent." This was the first time I had ever told anyone about that moment. It had always felt like maybe I had dreamed it but I knew I hadn't. The memory of it wasn't attached to anything—I didn't know what I'd been doing before I saw them or what happened afterward, I could only remember the moment I had stood in the doorway.

"That is gross. Why didn't you ever tell me that before?"

"I always forgot to."

"I get ill just hearing them do it."

"Yea, I know. I wish they were different. I wish they were like other people's parents."

"Can we go to sleep now, Misty?"

"Sure. I love you, Angie."

That was the one thing we did in our family. Before we'd go to bed we'd all say "Good night, I love you" to each other.

Angie said, "I love you too, Misty. Good night."

Then I'd get up and sit in the rocker. I would watch out the window, crying and praying for my parents to return or for the sun to come up.

Even though I was the oldest, Angie was the one who was never scared. She learned how to swim before me because she wasn't afraid of the water. She learned to ride her bike before me because she wasn't afraid to wreck. She climbed higher trees because she didn't think about falling. Angie wasn't afraid of ghosts, of the dark or to be alone. Still I felt responsible for her. I felt responsible for my mom and dad. I believed if I wasn't there my mom and dad would kill each other and Angie would disappear.

When all you want in life is to be protected it does something strange to you to have to be a protector. Maybe it was one of the things that made me be so scared all the time, because when you have to take responsibility for a lot of people so early on in life it makes you afraid that you aren't doing the right thing, especially when things aren't going so right.

When i entered high school I made myself quit being afraid for my parents and decided that instead of worrying and waiting I would spend as much time as possible away from them. Of course, my mom and dad had made a decision of their own. Now that I was at an age where I could get pregnant, stoned or drunk and soon I'd even be able to wreck their car they figured it was time to transform themselves into real parents. To them parenthood meant lots of rules, lots of punishment and staying home to get drunk as opposed to going out to bars.

When I was fourteen I fell in love with Joe Penny. Joe was a hippie, one of the few in our town. He had moved to Springfield to go to college. Teenagers I had met from bigger places always made time-machine jokes about Springfield. They'd say things like, "Shit, man. I got too stoned and set my time dial back ten years." Everyone would laugh and agree, especially the kids who had grown up in town.

There was a certain mix of bitterness and wistfulness in the local hippies I knew. I think it came from their frustration of knowing they were only an imitation of some picture they'd seen in a *Life* magazine. But at four-teen they were authentic enough to offer more excitement than anything else Springfield had to give.

All the college-age hippies hung out at a place called

Starship Landing. Starship Landing was three blacktop roads that dead-ended into three huge circles. They were way out in the country with nothing but hills and trees around them. Me and my then best friend Terry Sarris used to hitchhike out to the Landing. One day a van pulled over and picked us up. The guy driving was named Chico and he'd just gotten back in town from Mexico, where he said he spent every winter. He had long, curly black hair and pink-tinted, wire-rimmed glasses. The guy on the passenger side flashed us the peace sign as we crawled in back of the van. His name was Joe Penny and I fell in love with him as soon as he looked at me. Joe had blue-black hair that fell in waves down over his shoulders. He had bad posture and a T-shirt that said FILLMORE EAST. He was nineteen and had been to a sit-in in Washington, then hitchhiked to California to see Jimi Hendrix in concert. Joe and Chico were the first guys I had ever seen in person who had black hair or who had been to a real sit-in.

Chico and Joe didn't know the exact way to Starship Landing and me and Terry got all excited giving directions. "Turn here!" we'd scream out, trying to beat each other to the punch. One time we said it so far ahead of the turn that Chico swerved too soon and had to back up. He said, "Just one of you chicks give the signal." I let Terry give the rest of the directions and just listened while they all talked. Terry asked Joe what the sit-in was for.

"It wasn't for, it was against the war."

"Were a lot of people there?" she asked.

"Yea, it was incredible. Thousands of beautiful people," he answered.

"Were you at Woodstock?" she asked.

"I was there," Chico said.

"Oh wow, what was it like?" Terry had always wanted to meet someone who had been to Woodstock. Her bedroom was covered with posters and magazine pictures from the festival and when she thought she could get away with it she would tell people she had been there herself.

"I don't remember. I got too high," Chico said.

"Oh, well have you ever been to Haight-Ashbury?" she asked.

Chico tilted his head around to look at Terry, then him and Joe started laughing. "Hey are we gonna get thrown in jail for transporting you chicks over the city limits?"

"Here, this is the turnoff. Down this road," Terry yelled. Chico slammed on his brakes to keep from missing the road. Terry looked at me and grinned. Chico was having a hard time shifting the gears on his van, it kept making cranking, grinding sounds as he pulled onto the gravel. Chico was cussing his car out and talking to Joe about some kind of mechanical thing with the van. Terry looked at me and grinned. "Quick save," she whispered.

There were about fifteen people at Starship Landing. They all knew Chico and Joe and knew they had been on the road. People rolled special joints for them and gave them chunks of hash, and one girl, who was kind of overweight but practically naked, kept giving them shot guns and saying, "It's a great day for an orgy." I told Terry that if they started an orgy I was leaving. It wasn't because I believed it was bad but because I was too flat and I thought it would be really humiliating to be a wall-flower at an orgy.

Chico decided he liked Terry. Most all guys did because she was overdeveloped for her age. Even my grandfather, who was so straight and religious, would say, "She's a beautiful girl. That's what women are supposed to look like, not all bony the way they try to these days."

When it got dark Chico asked us if we knew a good place to swim. Terry and me had lived in this town our whole lives and knew all the best places to go, not like the college kids who were from out of town. We showed Chico how to get to Magraw's Ford, a place they'd never be able to find again without us.

Me and Terry had told our parents we were spending the night at each other's house so we didn't have to go home that night. When Joe asked what time I had to be in I said, "Whenever I want." I told him I was seventeen. We spent the whole night swimming and getting stoned and fooling around in the van. The next morning Chico dropped me and Terry off at the top of the hill from my house. We walked down the road in really high spirits.

I could always tell when something was off in my house. As soon as you opened the door it felt like you were entering another dimension. I was especially tuned in to disaster, though I hadn't learned to zone in on what kind of disaster. I couldn't tell if I was going to find someone dead or if I was going to get killed. Usually, though, I was so afraid for myself I'd start wishing someone had died. I figured at least that way I wouldn't be able to get in trouble for a year or so, especially if it was someone in the immediate family.

Me and Terry walked into the kitchen, she was still feeling good. Terry said, "Let's get your mom to fix us something to eat." There was my mom sitting at the table. I'd been hoping this feeling was just my imagination or guilt or something but when I looked at my mom's face I knew I was right again.

"Hey Mrs. Groves." Terry always called my mom that even though most everyone else called her by her first name. Calling my mom Mrs. Groves was Terry's way of being more intimate and my mom got off on this, so I was hoping Terry's presence would help me out of whatever situation I was about to be in.

"Terry, your parents called here last night looking for you. You better call and tell them where you are. They've been very worried." Me and Terry looked at each other. We were caught.

When Terry got off the phone she said, "My grandfather died. That's why they were trying to get a hold of me."

"Shit," I said.

My mom got all freaked out that I had cussed. She said, "I haven't told your father about this. If he knew you'd be in deep water. So I wouldn't add to your trouble." Blackmail, another maternal trademark. I felt like telling her to go on and tell my dad, that it was better than having her hold all my offenses over my head. But then I thought about what my dad would do and I realized blackmail was better.

My mom asked Terry if she needed a ride home.

"No. My mom's coming."

"I'm sorry you had to learn a lesson this way. If you need anything be sure and let us know."

"It's OK, he was really old and I didn't even know him hardly. I just hope I don't get grounded."

This was great. I could've kicked Terry. Now my mom would take Terry's lack of remorse out on me all day long.

After Terry left I cleaned my room and stood around my mom while she ironed clothes. I didn't say anything but I figured if I stood around her enough she'd start asking me questions about where I'd been and then we'd get in a fight and then she'd feel better. But she just concentrated on the clothes. I always knew when my mom was extremely upset because she ironed the sheets and my dad's handkerchiefs.

Before I went to sleep that night my mom came in my room. I thought she was going to tell me she loved me but she only said, "You'd never do those things if you thought your father would find out."

I started to deny it but it was true so I didn't. I could never understand why my mom took this so personal—

why she made me feel like I was proving I loved her less when all it meant was that I just wasn't so afraid of her as I was of my dad.

I went to sleep trying to think about being in the water with Joe but I kept flashing on my mom instead. No matter how much I wanted to think about my own life and having fun she always stood just to the side of everything.

Thinking I could escape, forget my mom and dad, I ran away from home for my second time. I left with much less preparation than I had when I was a kid. I just took the clothes on my back, hoping it would take longer for my parents to discover I was gone if nothing of mine was missing. I put on my hip-hugger, bell-bottom jeans, patterned with faces to look like the scene at Woodstock. And a shirt I had stolen at the mall. I would've bought it but it cost twenty-two dollars and I only had thirteen dollars on me. The shirt was a low-cut, sleeveless, velvet T-shirt, tie-dyed in shades of violet and lavender. I wore these clothes because I thought that if anything bad happened to me, like I died or something, or if anything good happened, like I met a cute guy, these would be the clothes I'd want to be remembered in.

I hitchhiked to Limberlost Park, which was the in-town extension of Starship Landing. When I got to the park the only person there was this guy named Rolo. He was always at the park but I hadn't ever talked to him because the first time I saw him he was eating live June bugs and grasshoppers. He was fat to begin with. I walked over to the picnic table he was sitting on.

"Has anyone been around?" I asked.

"Has anyone been around?" he said.

Rolo was that kind of guy. He tried to make girls hate him so he could feel like they hated him for a reason and not just because he was fat and gross. I felt sorry for him but not enough to not hate him.

"Have you seen Joe Penny?" I asked, even though I knew he wouldn't tell me.

"He's at the crash pad on Forsythe Alley. Know how to get there?"

"No."

"I'll take you over. But first you have to watch this," he said.

Rolo lit a cigarette, inhaled as deep as he could until his face was red and bloated; he dropped the cigarette, stuck his fingers in his ears and looked like he was going to explode, then smoke came drifting out of his eye sockets.

"What do you think?" Rolo asked, blinking his red, teary eyes.

"It looks like it hurts," I answered.

"It burns. But June bugs scratch your throat."

"Why do you do that junk?" I asked, sincerely curious.

"Because no one else does."

This was someone who would make my mom proud. She had this charleton side to her personality that came out every now and then. She'd say, "This is why I'm

stuck in this miserable town. I didn't have a gimmick."
She'd name off all the celebrities she thought were famous
from gimmicks they'd created. Marilyn Monroe (her
voice), Albert Einstein (his hair), Red Skelton (the way
he said good night). She had lists of people.

Rolo walked me over to Forsythe Alley. On the way
he asked if I was Joe's girlfriend. He said he liked Joe but
couldn't see what girls saw in him. Rolo said he had
crashed at Forsythe Alley himself before and that it was
a righteous place to stay. The crash pad was inside an old
apartment building. I hadn't been in that many apartment
buildings before. The hall floors were dirty tile and the
walls were painted a shiny, thick green. The apartment
was only one room, with a separate kitchen and bathroom. It was furnished with a lot of tapestries and sagging
furniture. There was a girl named Renora reading tarot
cards and a guy called Bean laying across the bed. They
were listening to the radio and talking about how unhip
all the local stations were. Bean kept saying, "I can't wait
to split this scene. This town is a burg."

I had met Bean before but he didn't remember me.
Terry and me had looked through the window of a house
that was near the college and seen orange silk material
draped from the ceiling. A van was parked in the driveway so we knew that hippies lived inside. We talked each
other into knocking on the door. A guy named China
Cat, with long, kinky hair, answered.

"We were wondering what's on your ceiling. We like
it," Terry said.

China Cat asked us in and said, "Curiosity is such a beautiful thing."

It was a parachute that hung across the ceiling, and there were pillows and bean-bag chairs on the floor. The place looked like a harem. Bean came out of the bathroom with a towel turbaned around his head saying, "That felt great. I haven't had a shower in six days."

China Cat rolled a joint and we all sat under the parachute. China Cat told us he was going to run for sheriff and he invited us to stay and eat so we could advise him with his campaign. Me and Bean walked to the Git-N-Go on the corner to get some macaroni and cheese. Before we left I started to put my shoes on but Bean said, "You don't need those."

Walking to the store I stayed on the street curb. I never liked going barefoot because I was afraid I'd step on a bee. Bean was barefoot and skating his feet through the grass, he noticed that I was staying on the pavement and said, "Only free spirits glide in the grass. I think you're one uptight chick."

I was glad he didn't remember me.

My first night at Forsythe Alley, Renora read my fortune with the tarot cards and said I was a seeker. The next night I was in the apartment by myself, I kept hoping I'd run into Joe because I hadn't seen him in over a month. A greasy-haired guy, who looked to be about thirty-seven, came in while I was playing with the tarot cards. He called himself Primrose. He was skinny and hunched over and looked like the guys who worked the rip-off booths at carnivals. He tried to sell me some hash, then asked me to do his fortune. I wanted him to leave me alone and as I got up to leave he said, "Wait, ssh, I hear someone. Sounds like cops. We better hide. I've got enough stash on me to get us busted for twenty years." Then he grabbed me and pulled me into a closet and told me to be still as he started trying to make out with me.

I heard voices in the other room and was afraid to come out of the closet or make any noise. Primrose forced me close to him. I felt too stupid to do anything, but tears were coming out of my eyes. Primrose started doing everything he wanted to me, then stopped when it was over. This was the first sex I'd had all the way. When he finished he said, "I recognize those voices, it's cool."

I came out of the closet after Primrose and tried to look different than I felt. Joe was sitting on the couch. I hadn't seen him ever look as good as he did. His hair was clean and he was wearing corduroys instead of jeans. He seemed like he looked older too. Joe asked me if I wanted to go for a walk. He bought me a sunflower burger at The Commune, the only health-food store in town. We walked over to the park, and he asked me if I knew Primrose and I said, "A little." Then Joe told me that Primrose was a narc and to stay away from him.

Other than the Primrose scene, the night was perfect. I was with Joe, I didn't ever have to go home and it was unseasonably cool. Joe told me that he had missed seeing me around and asked where I'd been. I had thought he was the one who wasn't around. Joe told me he knew of a treehouse we could sneak in.

In the treehouse I had sex for my second time and it made it seem like the first time had never happened at all. We were nervous about sleeping all night in the treehouse so we walked back to the crash pad. Every time a car drove by I was paranoid that it would be my dad but I didn't tell Joe because I didn't want him to know he had just had sex with a runaway.

At the apartment we sat around smoking Marlboros with Renora and Bean. Someone knocked at the door and I was hoping it wasn't Primrose but it was so late I figured he was coming to stay at the apartment. Joe opened the door and there was my dad and two policemen. I didn't have time to register anything but the look of surprise and fear on Joe's face as my dad dragged me out the door.

The policemen drove me home and my dad followed us in his car. I don't remember any of this ride. At my house me and my dad and my mom and the two policemen sat in the kitchen. They all sat at the table and I was on a bar stool that was under the wall phone. The phone was ringing and I wanted to answer it but I knew I wasn't allowed to act like this was my house.

The police started asking me questions—where I'd been, who I was with, did anyone give me drugs. My mom had obviously been crying the whole time I was gone. My dad told my mom to make some fresh coffee. They were already coffeed out of their minds.

My dad said, "You should have seen the place we found her at. It was filthy. Long-haired guys thrown out on the bed. The place was furnished with beds. Rubbers, used rubbers were laying on the floor."

"No one uses rubbers, you're lying," I yelled.

My dad reached over to hit me but then remembered the cops were there. "There were rubbers on the floor."

He was lying but I don't know if he knew it.

The police started asking me if I did drugs and what kind and how often. "Do you smoke marijuana?" the older cop asked, all questionnairelike.

"Sometimes," I said defiantly.

"How often?"

"Not very," I said as I watched my mom register deep relief. "I don't get high enough on grass," I added. My mom's face looked about ten years older than it had from the moment I walked in the door. She had looked so happy when the police led me into the kitchen, she cried, "You're safe, you're alive," and I had just looked at her like she was nuts.

"Do you smoke hashish?" the older cop asked, glaring at me.

"I have."

"Have you ever done hallucinogens?"

"Yes." My mom let out a cry.

"What kind?"

"Acid, mesc, mushrooms."

"How often have you done LSD?"

"I don't know."

"More than five times?"

"Twenty-five, maybe."

My mom was hysterical by this point but trying to maintain in front of the company. She was a mess. She cupped her hands over her mouth. "You can never have children," she cried.

"Who wants to?" I asked hatefully. I couldn't believe her. My mom couldn't have cared less if I never had kids, she was always saying never to do it, that kids would only make your life miserable.

My dad lit a cigarette and said to the cops, "Take her with you. I'm washing my hands."

I asked if I could say bye to Angie and my dad said he didn't want her to see me.

When we got out to the drive the older cop opened the door of the police car and said, "We'll be taking you down to juvenile hall. You'll be locked in detention with all the other delinquents."

"You'll have to stay over the weekend," the younger one said. "There's no paperwork Saturday and Sunday. But your dad can take you home Monday if he's cooled down by then."

The younger cop, whose badge read DIME, was standing between the two open doors on our side of the car. The older cop had his hand on my arm. I felt it tighten and pull me back up to a standing position.

"What do you mean, till he's cooled down? She's the

problem. Don't let her think any different. She's an incorrigible," the old cop said as he squeezed tighter on my arm.

Horror stories always circulated in school about kids being sent away to reform school for being incorrigible. No one knew anyone personally, but everyone claimed to know someone who knew someone that had been sent up.

If a girl who was kind of a loner but rumored to have a bad reputation disappeared for a while, everyone said she'd been sent to Chillicothe. If a hood was absent for more than a week he was suspected of being sentenced to Booneville. Chillicothe was the girls' reformatory and it was supposed to be even worse than Booneville, the boys' reform school. I think that was because nothing seemed scarier to people than a girl who wasn't afraid of things.

I believed that the girls in Chillicothe were always sneaking away to meet and make out with the boys from Booneville. They were about three hundred miles apart from each other but this never seemed like an obstacle to me. I started wondering if there would be any cute boys in the detention center. I figured at least there I'd meet someone who might understand me.

The policemen took the main strips of town to get to the detention center. As we pulled up to stoplights, the people in the cars next to us would stare over at me. I wondered what they thought I had done. Anytime I had ever seen anyone in the back of a police car I automatically thought they had murdered someone. If it was a man I believed he had probably murdered his wife. If I saw a woman in a police car I figured she had murdered her husband's girlfriend.

The cops in the front seat were talking about a guy in a Camaro they had pulled over earlier in the night on Kearney Street, who was going 120 mph.

"He really had souped up that piece of machinery. I hate giving tickets for crap like that. Beautiful car, ace driver," the older one said as he lit a Tareyton.

"Well it was his fault, all the dragsters know we have to ticket at the end of the month. He was trying to prove something."

"Maybe. Or else he was having trouble with his girl."

"He could've hit somebody," Dime said.

"You can't believe that, those guys have all been driving since they could reach the foot feed," the other cop said impatiently.

Kearney Street was the main drag of highway on the north side of town. It was the hangout for greasers, hot-rodders and hippie haters. It figured to me that cops liked to give these guys a break.

Being on Kearney Street was a time warp, it was like being in Thelma or Galena. Kearney could just as easily been the highway in front of my grandparents' house— the hot-rodder teenagers zooming back and forth, the screaming, shrieking girls and the sounds of breaking bottles.

I wished now more than anything that my grandparents had lived with us. I believed if my grandparents lived with us my parents wouldn't fight anymore because my mom never wanted them to know how our life really was. She believed the shock would kill my grandmother. My mom was a grown woman with a husband and two teenagers and she still hid from her parents the fact she drank and smoked cigarettes. I would've wished I could live with my grandparents except that life in Thelma would've been only slightly more exciting than my dad's vision of hell.

There was a time, though, I wanted to shock my grandmother or at least open her eyes. I knew I couldn't tell her how awful life at home was. I couldn't tell her about Mom and Dad's fights or how Mom couldn't get through more than a day without a pint of vodka. I couldn't tell her that we didn't really know if Dad lived at home with us or had some other house he lived at, with some other woman and some other kids. So instead I told her I didn't believe in God and for a few seconds she was so devastated it was almost as if I had said, "Mom's a drunk and they leave us alone for days and Dad beats us."

But, probably it kind of did mean the same thing to my grandmother, since she believed if you didn't believe in God that was all the stuff that happened to you anyway.

I started to feel bad about freaking my mom out. Telling her I had done acid so many times. Still, when I watched her reaction part of me had felt really happy. I felt honest and freed. She had seemed like such a hypocrite at that moment. For my whole life she had preached to me to never have kids, how they'll ruin your life. Even when she was happy or we were all having a nice day together, she'd manage to throw in how good days were few and far between when you had to depend on a whole family feeling good at the same time. I served her right to see that she had made her point, that I didn't care if I never had kids. Because the truth was I didn't ever want to be a parent, because it's parents who aren't good for kids. They're the ones who have kids to give something to their own lives, not to give their children lives of their own. And when their kids don't turn out the way the parents want, they only become a constant reminder and reflection of how selfish and unfit the parents were to start with.

And now I was wishing I would've taken better advantage of my police protection. I wish I would've said, "Officers, are you here to arrest my dad for beating up my mom? Or for the way he gets drunk and drives way over the speed limit? Or for the time he totaled out the bottom of his Thunderbird, then duped a poor sucker into buying it by forgetting to mention it was wrecked beyond repair? Or are you here to arrest him for always killing more than his limit of anything that can be hunted?"

At the detention center a big, fat woman gave me a new toothbrush, told me to take a shower and give her my clothes, then she handed me a blue gown and thongs. I was locked in a room that had bunk beds with wire mesh over the windows. A courtyard separated me from the men's county jail. Before my light was turned out I heard the prisoners yelling nasty things at me. It felt a lot different hearing these guys saying lewd things than it had when me and Celia would stand on the lawn in front of the mesh-covered windows of the Stone County courthouse. When the lady turned the keys to lock my door she said, "You're in solitary now."

"What's new?" I yelled as I kicked the door.

About four o'clock that morning I heard my door open and another girl was brought in. They did the same routine with her and I pretended I was asleep as she climbed into the top bunk.

Saturday morning, the fat woman brought us Rice Krispies and Kool-Aid. The girl downed her Kool-Aid, then said, "I wish this was electric." She told me her name was Betsy and that she got arrested holding a hundred hits of acid that her boyfriend had stuffed in her bra.

Betsy's boyfriend was Kimen Holder. Everyone knew him. Betsy was only sixteen and she seemed too pretty and clean-cut to be Kimen's girlfriend. He was a drug addict who beat up girls. It made me a little uneasy that he was her boyfriend.

At six o'clock the detention shift changed and two college boys took over. They brought us extra sandwiches for dinner and said they'd let us out after the little kids were in their rooms. At ten-thirty they let us come out and watch TV in the group room. They had us give them massages and let us smoke cigarettes and play cards.

I really liked the boys. They were like the lifeguard at Arden Pool. They were less experienced than the other people I knew. They didn't do drugs or have sex or get bad grades. They probably ate dinner every night in the same chair at the kitchen table. These boys would have been surprised and thrilled and intimidated by the things I could tell them. They would feel the same towards me as I did to the people I had been hanging around.

Around two A.M. they said we'd have to go back to our room. After I was in bed and almost asleep Betsy crawled down in my bunk and started kissing me, she said she had gotten turned on giving the boys massages. Betsy told me I didn't have to do anything but lay there and that she'd stop anytime I said so. I never said anything and the next day the same thing happened all over—the extra food, TV, massages, cigarettes and Betsy.

On Monday the fat lady was back. When she came to clear our breakfast trays she said, "Your parents are in the visiting room."

"Good luck, baby," Betsy said as I followed the fat lady.

When my mom looked at me in the blue gown she started crying. My dad asked, "Well have you learned your lesson?" Then he said, "The only reason I'm bringing you home is for your mother."

When we got home my mom said I should take a nice hot shower and my dad ordered me to give him the clothes I was wearing.

"I'm going to burn these and there will be no more of this kind of hippie junk coming into the house. This is what the problem is. I never should have let you start wearing these things. And next I'm getting rid of all that music," he said, pointing to my stereo and albums. "It all influences you to think this kind of crap is OK. They tell you to run away."

"I didn't run away because of a stupid record or a pair of pants."

"You better talk to me with a little more respect from now on too. I don't want to hear that tone of voice again."

"What're you gonna beat it out of me?"

"Please let's all stay calm," my mom pleaded. "Just let her get in the shower. We can talk about the clothes and the records later. Let's just try and have a nice day."

"Well, I'm burning those clothes," my dad said, "so hand them over. Now."

"But this is my favorite shirt. It's beautiful to me."

"I don't care. I don't ever want to see them on you again."

"I won't wear them. Please let me keep them though. I love them. I want to have them when I'm old."

"You don't have to worry about getting old. Not the way you're headed."

I thought about all my mom's clothes that she had saved from when she was young. Dresses like no one made anymore. Dresses with sequins and rhinestones. She had big hoop skirts and dresses that were tight and glittery like she had imagined big-city women wore to fancy cocktail parties. She still had high heels that were in their original shoeboxes. My favorites were peacock-blue suede with a big suede rose that had a pink fake-diamond in its center. The thin spiked heels were ribboned black and silver. My mom even had the hats she had worn. Hats with jewels, flowers, ribbons or veils, hats as glamorous as the hatboxes she stored them in.

Me and Angie had played dress-up in these clothes. I'd listened to my mother tell me stories about them—the day she bought particular ones, the first place she had worn them, what she had thought about when she had them on.

I had started crying and felt like I would kill myself if my dad burned my shirt and jeans. "I'm begging you, Dad. Please don't take these away."

"No discussion. Hand them over," he demanded.

That afternoon my mom came in my room and turned on my TV. She said, "*Snake Pit* is on. It's such a scary movie, let's watch it."

Her and my sister sat on my bed with me to watch the movie. My mom had a thing about stories involving crazy people. She was always reading books like *I Never Prom-*

ised You a Rose Garden, Lisa and David or *The Bell Jar.*

My dad walked in my bedroom and looked around at us, "What are you watching?" he asked.

"*Snake Pit.* It's a movie about a lady in an insane asylum," Angie said. "Watch with us."

My dad laughed and said, "I don't need any movie to show me what nuts are like. I'm cooped up with three."

"You're an asshole," I said, walking over to slam my door on him.

My mom saw my dad's fist coming at me and screamed, "Will!" She caught me just as he knocked me over.

"I hate you," I said, looking him straight in the face.

"Leave her alone," my mom pleaded. "She doesn't know what she's saying, she's been through an ordeal this weekend."

I started laughing so hard that my mom freaked out. She thought the punch had addled something in my head and was trying to force me to lie down on the bed. I really wanted to tell her what kind of weekend I'd had. My dad walked down the hall mumbling, "You're all crazy."

After that summer vacation I started my sophomore year of high school. I think Betsy ended up in Chillicothe, but she didn't have any real parents. I heard that Joe got arrested for publishing an underground newspaper. I also heard he had moved back to St. Louis to live with his family and go to school there.

SOPHOMORE YEAR WAS the year teachers had decided it was important that you knew what you wanted to do with your life and important for them to feel like they had some involvement in it. I still didn't have much use for my teachers, it felt like all they wanted was to make sure you followed the rules and knew the dates of deaths of presidents, treaty signings and wars. Teachers didn't seem so concerned with what you wanted to learn so much as if you learned what was in their school manuals.

Stuart Kyle and me shared the same homeroom—English composition. Stuart didn't like the class because he only cared about cars, car parts and how to earn extra money. I thought I could like English, but I couldn't stand our teacher, Mrs. Oliver. She was short and skinny and had ghost-white skin with even whiter blotches on it. Every time she'd get nervous or mad in class her skin would melt into bright red patches on her neck and arms and her eyes would get weepy. She got angry quick and couldn't take a joke at all. The students really liked to tease her and her skin was their meter of success.

One of our first assignments from Mrs. Oliver was to write a composition about an experience we had we believed no one else had had. Mrs. Oliver said it should be an experience where we learned something about ourselves. She added that our paper should contain honest and revealing insights into our real feelings. And then she said, "Take a chance with this!" as she popped her fist out in front of her enthusiastically. This was the first project since I'd started high school that I was excited to do.

I wrote:

Billy held me while I slept through the end of the heroin. My arms were still dried with blood in places. I felt him hold me a long time before I could go to sleep.

We were warm, the sun was almost starting to come in. It was a big, old house we were in, with glass that was stained different colors and pinwheels carved above the doorways. We were in the upstairs, that's where Billy's room was, it was like an attic room almost and one other boy lived across the hall but he was never around. A girl lived downstairs in a room that was kind of like a porch with windows all around, a day porch some old person would have called it. I don't even know how it came to happen really but there I was and now I was upstairs with Billy. He hadn't even talked to me that much before, except to say some little-sister type stuff—"You were out awful late last night," "That guy looked like trouble," "You shouldn't spend so much time next door, that girl's bad news."

He was a lot older than me, he was twenty-one. He had never done it with a needle before. Billy said he had to keep reminding himself how young I was, I said it made me mad when people said I was young. We wanted to feel the heroin again. So I cooked some more in the spoon. I felt like he didn't think I was so young now. I did it to myself first and then I did it to him. It was easy because he was a boy and his veins were big. We breathed deep and I felt my throat get this certain taste then get numb and tickly. I went downstairs and got sick and took a Pepsi out of the refrigerator. I drank some and got sick again but I still felt really good then I went back upstairs and Billy opened the second pack of cigarettes we had, we smoked a lot of cigarettes. We sat in front of the stereo and played records. Billy said Lou Reed was the greatest and I listened to all the words. I laughed while we played Sally Can't Dance, but it wasn't the kind of laugh I had when my sister would tell me a joke, it was low and tired. I remembered old women in bars laughing that way. I used to go to a lot of bars when I was little. I had been going since I was a baby because my dad would carry me with him. I used to make up stories about every person in those bars but a lot of the women stories ended up the same.

Billy asked me what I was thinking.

"Nothing," I answered.

"I wish we had enough to lay in bed all day," Billy said and it made me feel stronger than him, or more powerful because I knew I could get him to stay in bed all day, without even using my body.

Billy had a rich mom and dad and went to college and didn't have to work. He said he knew what he was going to be. He had a hundred dollars in a cigar box that his grandma had given him for nothing, just because she came and saw him. So we decided to get more heroin with it. It was still too early so we did the rest we had then Billy went and warmed up the car and we put on a bunch of sweatshirts and threw a blanket in the car and went driving around. We drove out in the country and the frost was just starting to glisten and melt so it made a blur against the sun. Maggie May was playing on the radio so Billy turned it up. We started driving towards Mill River. It was pretty early in the morning so it was real quiet. We passed two deserted cars then pulled over. I rolled a joint and Billy said he wished he had his Bowie tape in the car. But the only ones he had were too wrong for our mood so we just kept the radio turned low till a good song would come on. It was so cold it was hard to tell the difference between our breath and the smoke.

I felt like I should be getting ready to go to school, this is where I was supposed to be at this time, trying to finish some last-minute homework in the parking lot between hits off a joint, waving to someone on their way to class.

I felt depressed so I tried not to think about anything bad. I looked at Billy, he was somewhere else too—thinking about the girlfriend he probably had and wondering if anyone would find out what he had done. Billy had said he wanted to waste his whole day doing dope and doing me. Waste, I was going to spend my day doing that. I wondered if I'd be like one of those old women who only married men would want to see.

People had always thought I was too wild but I didn't feel wild. I wasn't reckless, I didn't do things with abandon. I might not have been sure why I did the things I did. But I was sure why I didn't do some things. It was like I was hitch-hiking through life and would get in any interesting car that would pull over for me. But as soon as I didn't like the direction I was heading I was out. I really just wanted to find a ride I could stay with for the whole way.

I was proud of my paper. I did everything the teacher had asked. It sounded like a story to me, it was long enough and I had definitely taken a chance. I even bragged to my parents that I was probably going to get an A.

The day Mrs. Oliver handed our papers back she said, "I don't think any of you tried very hard. The punctuation was sinful." As she walked through the aisles she looked over at me the whole time. When she got to my desk she held my paper by the corner high above my head with the tips of her thumb and forefinger. "You can all thank Misty Groves, though. Since I grade on a curve she insured you all received A's," she said as she dropped my paper on my desk. There was an F on the top of it and a written note saying she only wished her garbage disposal had been working. Then she said, loud enough for the whole class to hear, "If I believed for a second any of this could be true you would be in the principal's office waiting for the police. For punishment I should make you read it aloud to the class but I don't think it would be fair to them to have to listen to it."

I fingered her as she walked away.

After class a few of the kids asked if they could read my paper but I told them I had already thrown it out.

Me and Stuart would skip class two mornings a week and that was how we first got together. By October we were spending every night we could together. On school nights he came over and we'd sit in my family room and watch TV or sit out on the front porch and talk. On weekends we'd go to the drive-in, sneak in empty houses that were up for sale or go to the river. One night we went to a river party. Me and Stuart were hanging out downstream from the other kids, who were building a fire up on the bank. It was starting to get dark and we walked into the river and stood under this manmade waterfall. The water fell in front of us and the mist from the falls wetted our skin. Stuart put his mouth on my neck and said he could tell from the taste there was a lot of black bass in the stream. Then Stuart told me he loved me and would for as long as we lived. Stuart said he couldn't wait until we were old enough to live together and we would fantasize often about that. Stuart would say, "We can get a place out in the country and have parties every night that we feel like it. I could work on my car all day long."

"We could take showers together every morning. We could do it all the time. We could lay in bed together all day. I'd cook cakes and pies and macaroni and cheese," I would ramble on, seeing the picture get clearer and bigger in my head. But as the picture seemed to get more involved for me, Stuart would drift away. His eyes would look far off. I figured he was probably thinking about cars and fishing and football. At those time I wished I had something I liked to think about too, instead of just wondering about what Stuart was thinking.

One weekend my mom made me go with her and Angie to visit my grandparents. It was the weekend I had planned to tell my parents I was sleeping at Laura Campbell's house and she was telling her parents she was staying with me. Then we were going to spend the whole night at Hayward Vincent's house with Stuart and Laura's boyfriend, Jed Holbrook.

Hayward's parents were always away on trips to foreign places and usually he had some other relative in to stay with him. But for one whole weekend he had the house completely to himself. Stuart and Jed had already bought beer and rum so that me and Laura could make piña coladas. I was mad about having to go all the way to my grandparents' and complained for most of the two-hour drive. My mom and Angie tried to cheer me up and finally Angie got mad and said, "She just wants to be home so she can go to a party at Hayward Vincent's house and screw Stuart."

"You little slut. You better shut your mouth," I yelled as I punched Angie in the arm.

"Why do you girls say things like that to one another? It's mean," my mom said.

"She's a slut, she's the one who's screwing Stuart. Everyone knows," Angie said as she punched me back in my arm.

"I'm not screwing anyone," I said. Which was true because even though me and Stuart had been together for seven months now we had only gone all the way one time. We would make out and fool around but we had only done it that one time. It bothered me, especially since things weren't so great between me and Stuart any-more. We didn't ever talk and he hadn't told me he loved me since Christmas.

"You just better shut your mouth, slutface, before I shut it for you," I yelled in her face.

"Mom!" Angie screamed, making it a four-syllable word.

"Stop it! Stop it right now. We're going to be at your grandparents' soon and I don't want them to see you all fighting."

"Why not? We're such hypocrites. They should know by now how we live," I said.

My mom slammed on the brakes so hard that Angie almost fell into the front seat. I banged my head against the windshield.

"Listen here, you spoiled little brat. I'm sick and tired of you wanting your way all the time. You think this world was made for your enjoyment? I don't know why I can't ever get what I want from anyone. All I'd like is one day of peace. I've been listening to you complain for this entire drive."

My mom was screaming and digging through her purse to find her cigarettes. She lit up a Salem. I hated the smell of those worse than any brand I'd ever smelled. I wanted to roll the window down but I was afraid she'd get more upset.

I was afraid of my mom in such a different way than I was of my dad. With my dad I was afraid because he got so mad at me. But with my mom I was afraid because when she got mad, she got mad about the whole world.

The highway to Thelma curved all the way, right up to the long stretch that was the town. As my mom squealed the tires around each curve I just sat there frozen, with tears dripping down my face.

"What're you crying for? You got what you wanted. We're all miserable now," my mom yelled.

As we rounded one of the curves a package liquor store came into view; my mom swerved the car into the gravel lot.

Me and Angie didn't say a word to each other while she was inside because we knew if we did she would somehow know everything we had said and get even more mad at us.

When she got back in the car she opened a jar of orange-flavored vodka and poured it into a flask she kept in her purse. Then she chugged the vodka from the flask until her eyes watered. She was already drunk by the time she started the car.

"And if you say or do one thing to upset Mom and Dad with any of your ideas you'll be the sorriest girl alive, Misty," my mom said in a threatening slur.

When we got to my grandparents' my mom greeted them with a sickening grin. She kept saying, "Now we just made a quick trip today, Mom. We've got to leave soon. Our little precious has a special school function tonight. We can't let her miss that." Then my mom would look at me so that I could know how much she really hated me.

My grandmother kept asking my mother if she was OK until my mom finally got mad and yelled, "Of course, of course I am, Mom. Why wouldn't I be? I've got two lovely girls. An honorable, trustworthy, loving husband. Parents who love me and always wish the best for me. Why wouldn't I be OK?"

I didn't know if my grandparents even knew how bad they had messed up my mom's life. But I knew because my mom told me all the time. Even though I loved my grandparents so much, sometimes it made me feel good to hear some of her problems were their fault instead of mine. My mom had never forgiven them for them wanting her to marry my dad and be a teacher when what she really wanted was to be something glamorous in a far-away place.

It was a pretty terrible day but after lunch my mom sobered up a little and then we left. As soon as we were a mile out of Thelma my mom started speeding again. Nobody said anything and I just tried to concentrate on the fun I'd be having that night, to keep me from wondering if we'd all live that long.

When Laura came over that night my dad took us out for ice cream before he dropped us at Jed's house.

Before we left my house I kissed my mom and tried to tell her I was sorry, but all she said was that my granma and granpa didn't have long to live.

When we got to Jed's, his parents gave us each a glass of wine and we watched Andy Griffith. While we waited for Stuart we whispered about the beer and piña coladas.

My stomach had butterflies and when I watched Jed kiss Laura I felt nervous. I wished Stuart would hurry.

It was almost eight. I wondered if Stuart was OK or if he was not coming. I thought maybe he had gotten in trouble for something and his parents weren't going to let him out of the house. I asked Laura again if she had for sure talked to Stuart. Then I wondered if he had decided to go out with another girl. He wasn't ever late when we were first together.

I had never been good at waiting, the whole time I would have images of what terrible things could be happening that would keep someone from being somewhere they said they would be. It always felt exactly the same as waiting for my parents to come home on those nights they had promised to be back by midnight. The reasons I had in my head were different reasons than the ones I imagined for my parents but my body had the same tightness and anxiousness I would feel sitting in the rocker in my parents' front room.

Then there was a tap at the glass doors. Jed opened the curtains and there was Stuart standing hunched over with a cigarette hanging out of his mouth.

Stuart came in and stood by me but he didn't give me a kiss. I was still upset from all the things I had been thinking and now I felt really bad. When I asked him what took him so long he said, "Nothing," and started dancing around saying he felt in form and was ready to party.

Jed held Laura closer and they started whispering in

each other's ear. Stuart started bopping like a boxer to his reflection in the sliding glass. I couldn't wait until me and Stuart were alone so I could ignore him, especially when he finally did try to kiss me.

I had looked forward to Hayward's party since I'd first known about it. I had planned for it, dreamed of it and had an awful day because of it. It seemed typical that the party turned out to be a bust. Hayward's parents had come back from out of town and only five other kids had shown up. Stuart brought me home early that night and I never even got a chance to ignore him.

It was almost summer. During Christmas vacation me and Stuart had talked about how great summer vacation would be. Instead of two weeks we would have three whole months to be together for full days, not just a couple of hours here and there. But as the days got warmer Stuart got colder and colder. Anytime I would try and ask him if anything was wrong he'd just say, "Don't know what you mean."

Sometimes me and Stuart would double-date with Marcie Jennings and Howie Cleaver. Marcie and Stuart were next-door neighbors and Stuart had gotten to be friends with Howie. I didn't like them—Marcie acted like a parent, she had an opinion or a complaint about every-thing. And Howie was just a fool. Every time he would smoke a joint he'd hyperventilate before each hit. He said it made you get higher. But he must not have known how stupid he looked, bending over and gasping for air eight or ten times before each puff he took.

On one of our double dates we bought beer and snuck in a sale house to get drunk. A while later me and Stuart went out for more beer. When we got back to the house we walked in to find Howie and Marcie completely naked.

The time me and Stuart had sex was the first time I had ever had sex with someone my own age and who I knew for a fact I would see again the next day. As much as I always wanted to have sex, though, I had never had that great of a time at it yet. With Joe Penny I thought I really liked it but I realized later that it wasn't so good because I had been so freaked out by the thing that had happened before with Primrose.

When me and Stuart did it he breathed really hard and made grunting noises, while he pumped up and down so fast and crazy I didn't know how he could feel anything. Then he ahhed and wriggled and pulled himself up fast and just as fast he collapsed right down on top of me. He had tears that were dripping down my cheeks and there was wet, milky stuff on my stomach. I felt sticky all over. I think Stuart didn't know I was still there, he felt the way someone would feel that had just dropped dead on you. I dipped my finger down and tasted what was dripping down my side.

As I looked at Marcie on her knees and Howie standing facing her I remembered the time I had tasted what was

on my stomach. At least Stuart was sexy. I couldn't imag-
ine how awful it would taste with someone like Howie.
Even though I didn't like her, all I could think was, Poor
Marcie.

Two weeks before summer vacation Stuart came to
school with some mushrooms he had blended up in a
quart of Tropicana. We decided to skip classes until lunchtime because Stuart had to be back in time for a special
project he had in shop. As we were going out to the
parking lot to drink the Tropicana and drive to the river
we ran into Laura and Jed and Tammy Unsuen and Tim
Withers. They had all just eaten acid and were trying to
figure out where to go. Stuart was the only one of us
who had a car. We all wanted to go to Lindenlure but
Stuart said we only had time to go to Peckers Beach.

No one really hung out at Peckers Beach because you
couldn't swim there. It had muddy, diseased water that
was filled with snakes and snapping turtles. But it was
close to school, so it was the place to go if you were only
going to skip a class or two or had to be home early from
school. By the time we were halfway there I couldn't stop
giggling and my body felt like it was made out of a rubber
eraser.

A big open field with two huge walnut trees stood in
the field across the road from the river. We were all walking single file, staring at our feet as we crossed the road,
and suddenly Jed yelled out, "Shit, man. Check it out!"

We all looked up except for Laura, who was trying to

figure out how to get her shoelaces tied. A man was hanging by a rope from one of the walnut trees.

"A dead man," Tammy said.

Laura stood up and looked over at the tree. "Maybe he isn't dead," she said.

We climbed through the barbed-wire fence and pushed each other to the tree like we were walking through a haunted house. As we stood in front of the hanging man we looked from him to each other.

"He's dead for sure," Tim said. "He looks really strange."

"Look at his tongue is hanging out. It looks too long," Laura said, staring at his tongue.

"Maybe that's why he hung himself. He couldn't go on living with long tongue disease," Jed said as Tammy giggled.

"Maybe he didn't kill himself. Maybe someone killed him and maybe that person is still here," I said.

Laura started screaming, "Let's get out of here."

Jed laughed. "Don't you want to hang around with him?"

"I'm scared. I want to go," she said louder.

"Be cool. Misty was just trying to freak us out. The only hangman around here is hanging from that tree," Stuart said.

"I'm not trying to freak anyone out, Stuart. You don't know if he killed himself," I said, hating the way he seemed to put me down so much these days.

"It's pretty obvious," he said.

"Maybe we're hallucinating him," Tammy said.

"I don't think everyone has the same trip, Tam," Stuart answered as he walked over and swung the man's body. "He's stiff. This is too weird. Touch him."

"No way!" me and Laura screamed at the same time. We jumped and grabbed hold of each other.

"What are we gonna do?" Laura asked, her body shivering against mine.

"Does anyone know him?" asked Tim.

"If we call the cops they'll know we're stoned," Jed said.

"Yea and if we tell anyone at school we'll get caught for skipping," Tammy replied.

"I can't afford to get caught again. I'll get suspended, then I'll be up shit creek," Tim said.

"Maybe we'd be heroes for finding the guy," I added.

"Maybe they'll think we did it," Laura cried.

I didn't feel stoned at all anymore. I felt different than I ever had. My body couldn't move, my brain was numb, but not from the mushrooms. Tammy started crying uncontrollably and saying she was having a bad trip. "I can't believe this. I don't know if he's dead or if he's a dummy or if you're all here or if I'm here or if I'm here alone and seeing you all here or if I'm alive or . . . where I am. Maybe I'm still walking by the river and I'm hallucinating this and I'm hallucinating you telling me I'm not hallucinating. Maybe I'm having a freakout and I'm really in a hospital right now. How do I know this is happening? How do I know any of this is happening? How will I know when it isn't happening anymore if it ever happened at all? Maybe this is all life is. You all might not be here really . . ." Tammy kept on going.

"She's having a bummer," Jed said. "We better get her out of here."

"Someone has to talk her down," Stuart said. He was always the responsible one in these situations. I thought that was because he was so job-oriented.

Tim volunteered, "I'll take her over to my house. No one's home. We'll just stay there until she comes down."

"We've gotta get back to school," Stuart said.

"What about the guy?" Laura asked.

"Someone else will find him. A million people drive through here. It's not like we're gonna be able to do anything for him now," Jed told us.

We got in the car and Tammy babbled all the way to Tim's house. But even after she was out of Stuart's car I couldn't stop hearing what she was saying.

That night after dinner Laura called me at home. Me and Stuart were sitting in my family room watching *The Mod Squad*.

"Did you watch the news?" Laura asked.

"No."

"They found a man who hung himself at Peckers Beach."

"No kidding."

"My parents might be able to hear me," she whispered. "Yea they found a man who hung himself at Peckers Beach. Isn't that weird?"

139

"Truly," I said as I signaled to Stuart. "They found the guy," I whispered to him.

"The news said he was a drifter and that he had a note in his pocket that said he couldn't go on anymore. Isn't that sad?"

"Think of the poor people who found him," I said.

"I know, it must've been awful. You know who found him?"

"Who?"

"Jenny Bancroft and Mark Southern. They told the police they were going over to Jenny's house to get homework they had left there the night before so their teacher wouldn't get mad at them."

"We should've said that."

"Six people don't generally forget their assignments," she whispered back into the phone.

"I've gotta go. Stuart's here. You OK though?"

"Yea."

"Have you heard from Tammy?"

"I talked to Tim. He said she's cool but that she's really bummed out."

"That's a drag."

"He said he had to really work on her to keep her from telling her parents."

"Well, see ya tomorrow."

"Meet me in the parking lot early," Laura said.

"OK. See ya."

When I hung up the phone all I could think about was

Tammy and the things she had said. Even though I knew she was stoned and having a bad trip, it all made total sense to me. I knew why she wanted to tell her parents. I wanted to tell mine too. I always wanted to tell them everything there was to know about my life, about who I was and what I did and where I went. But I knew I couldn't because they would freak out. Not being able to tell them these things made my life feel the way Tammy was saying. I didn't know what was real, my life they saw or the one I had to keep hidden from them.

On the last day of school that year Stuart drove me home. While we were sitting in his car in my driveway, he told me he was going to be real busy for a while and we wouldn't be able to see each other as much. Tears welled in my eyes as I asked him what he meant. He said, "Well we'll probably see each other as much, but we can't go out tonight."

"But it's the last day of school. We were going to celebrate tonight," I said, barely able to speak.

"I know. Well I've got to go now," he said as he reached across me to open the car door. "See ya," he said, without even looking over at me or waving bye as he backed out of the drive.

The next day Stuart didn't call and two days later I called him. His brother answered the phone and I could hear him whispering my name; then he said, "Sorry, he's not here." A week later I called Stuart and he answered the phone because I guess he had forgotten me so much he'd even forgotten to avoid me. I asked, "What's going on?"

Stuart said that he was in a hurry but that things were still the same and he'd call me later. He never called me again and I was miserable for the whole summer. Jed and Laura broke up too, but at least he told her about it and he still called her every once in a while. But me and Laura decided that guys weren't good for anything and mimicking Stuart we'd say, "At least girls are good for one thing."

It took me a long time to get over Stuart. I wanted to call him and tell him how much I hated him and how he had hurt me. I wanted to tell him I had never loved him and how bad the one time we finally did do it was. How he made stupid noises and moved like a fish flopping around in a net. I wanted to scream, "Fuck you, you fucker, motherfucker fucking coward. How much balls does it take to say I'm breaking up?" I hated Stuart more than I had hated anything. But I didn't call him because I knew if I did I'd just remember how much I loved him. How sexy his voice was and how he really was the best kisser of anyone I had ever kissed.

Later that summer Laura heard from Jed that Stuart was going to marry Marcie Jennings because he had gotten her pregnant. I figured if I lived next door to Stuart that would be me instead. Hearing about Stuart getting married made me feel terrible and I started crying like it was the first day I had realized Stuart was not ever going to be with me again.

In these situations my mom would try to be a comfort to me, she'd sit next to me and cradle her arms around me and rock me like I was a baby. During these times my mom was this combination cynic and wise man. I didn't know which of them I mistrusted most but I guess I liked the wise man side to her least—her voice would soothe out and she'd quote proverbs she'd read from these ornate, miniature, ancient proverb books she kept laying around the house.

But my mom was most comfortable with the cynic. She believed the wise man so little by the time she was trying to lay it on me it felt phony to both of us. Still, you end up absorbing some of it, so it was good she tried telling me about seashells on the seashore and time healing all wounds and how into each life some rain must fall to make it rich and fertile, before she'd say, "You'll get over it. Soon enough you'll wonder what you ever saw in him. You wonder that eventually even if you stay together, so it's better to be rid of him by the time you don't know why you're not."

LAURA CAMPBELL HAD been one of my best friends off and on since junior high. She was the first person I ever snuck out with. In junior high sneaking out of your parents' house after midnight was a big deal. The first time we had planned to sneak out was on a school night. The whole day at school we talked about how we were going to paper Steve Taylor's house. Laura was going to set her alarm for eleven-thirty, get four rolls of toilet paper from her bathroom, then come knock on my bedroom window. That night I was extra nice to my parents. I helped my mom load the dishwasher and I sat with my dad while he watched the news. Before I went to bed I kissed them both and told them I was lucky to have such great parents.

When I got in bed I read *Mademoiselle* magazine and tuned in my radio to the top ten countdown, then slid it under my pillow to keep me awake.

The next morning my mom came in and woke me for school. She pulled my covers back and said, "You seem awful sleepy, Misty. Did you have a rough night?"

Just then I remembered my and Laura's plan. I figured that she must've fallen asleep too, since she hadn't come over.

"We had company last night. They tried to wake you but you know how deep you sleep."

"Who came?" I asked. My mom seemed in too good a mood to know about me and Laura but she had tricked me this way before, trying to make me think everything was OK.

"Oh it was so late I didn't want to force you out of bed."

I figured my dad must've gone out late and come back

drunk with some of his friends. Every once in a while he would decide he wanted to have the family around him or show us off to his friends, but it was always three or four in the morning when he'd do this. He'd drag us out of bed and force us to sit at the kitchen table with him and eat pizza he had brought home. Then he'd get mad at us because we were so tired all we would want to do would be to go back to sleep.

Once Angie refused to eat the pizza he had brought in. She stood up from the table to go back to bed. "This is stupid. Just 'cause you're drunk and hungry you're gonna make me listen to your bar stories and eat soggy pizza," she said, then started to walk away.

Angie had long hair down to her waist. My dad grabbed her hair and yanked her back into her chair. "You sit your butt down there and don't move a muscle," he yelled.

I would have been crying and trying to reason with him if it had been me but Angie just sat there with a blank stare on her face. A few minutes later she said flatly, "I'm sick of you pulling my hair. Don't ever do it again."

My dad started laughing and slurred, "You think you're gonna tell me what to do or not do to you. Why hell, you're my property, punk. And don't you forget it."

Angie didn't say another word, even though my dad kept trying to make her answer "Yes sir."

My mom was pleading the whole time, saying, "Will, don't."

Finally he ordered me and my mom to leave and he made Angie stay sitting in the chair. After my dad passed out my mom led Angie back to her bed.

The next morning when me and Angie were in the bathroom getting dressed for school Angie shut and locked the door. She took out the scissors my mom kept in her makeup drawer and cut off her hair in four big chunks up to her ears.

People had always said that Angie had the most beautiful hair they'd ever seen. It was long and light brown with golden wisps, and it waved and curled into locks at the ends. It was so soft and shiny, strangers would ask if they could touch it.

Angie's hair laid on the bathroom floor in a heap at her feet.

"Angie, why did you do that?" I asked. I was kind of in shock. Angie had long hair her whole life and for the first time I was seeing her with hair shorter than most of the boys at school. Plus it was the most terrible haircut in the world.

"Because it's my property," she said. Angie had tears, but she didn't let them drip down her face.

Angie was that way. I would've cried and apologized to my dad for saying the wrong thing to him and the next day I would let him be nice to me. Angie wouldn't ever say she was sorry to him.

I used to wonder why my dad never hit Angie but knocked the shit out of me for anything. But by this time I had realized it was because my dad knew he would have to kill Angie, since no matter how bad he hurt her she wouldn't tell him what he wanted to hear.

I couldn't wait to see my mom and dad's face when Angie came out of the bathroom. My mom would be so freaked out, she'd be crying and asking Angie what she had done. Sometimes these kinds of things made me feel sorry for my mom but usually they just made me mad at her. I thought it was as much her fault as it was my dad's that he did the things he did to us.

"You're really gonna show them. I'm sorry about your hair, though, Angie. Are you all right?"

"I guess. It'll be worth it. He can't yell at me to get it out of my face anymore, either."

"What do you think he'll do?"

"Have a coronary I hope," Angie said dryly.

"Dream on."

My mom started knocking on the bathroom door. "I need in, girls."

"Hold on," I yelled back.

"C'mon, it's getting late. I've got to fix my hair," she said.

Me and Angie started sweeping up all her hair and putting it in a plastic bag. "Wait till she yells long enough to get dad's attention. That way we'll get to catch them both at once," I whispered.

"OK."

"I'm going to count to ten, then I'm going to get your father," my mom said, trying to sound threatening.

I hated that voice because it sounded so fake. Just then

my dad came up. "What's going on? Do I have to hear all this yelling first thing in the morning?"

"Nothing's the matter. I just need to get in the bathroom," my mom said in her fake calm voice.

"Open the goddamn door. Now!" he shouted.

Me and Angie grinned and A-OK'd each other as we took our positions to open the door. We stood in front of the bathroom counter, facing the mirror and combing our hair. I felt excited as I opened the door. "It wasn't even locked," I lied, trying to make it sound like they were making a big deal over nothing.

Immediately my mom and dad's expressions froze. Not a sound came out of their mouths for what seemed like ten minutes. It was beautiful. Then all of a sudden my dad looked over at me. "What in the hell did you do to her?" he screamed at me.

"She didn't do it. She didn't do anything. I did it myself. I can do things by myself, you know," Angie said.

My mom was right on schedule, tears, pleas, and "oh whys." Then suddenly my dad reached his arm out and slapped me hard as he could across my face. It stung and tears automatically came to my eyes. "You influenced her. This is your fault," he said.

"I hate you. This is your fault, you stupid idiot," Angie said as she pushed her way past him.

"Get in here. I'm not through with you," he shouted.

"Fuck you," she said as she slammed the door to her bedroom behind her.

"This is all because of you," my dad yelled. "You

brought drugs into this house. You ran away to hang out with trash. I'm holding you responsible."

"You're a joke." I laughed. "You're the one everything's because of, you and mom."

My dad reached over and hit me again. "You tell me this was all your fault right now."

I hated my dad, especially because my face was hurting so bad. I remembered all the times he had caught me off guard, asking me with concern, "Does your face hurt?" I'd look in his eyes and wonder what he was seeing, what was on my face to make him think that and I'd say, "No," hesitantly.

"Well it's killing me," he'd say laughing, proud of himself that he had tricked me again with the same joke.

"Tell me you're responsible for this," he screamed as he swung at me again, his hand landing where my face was already numb.

My dad was totally hysterical and Angie was at the point she'd risk anything to make him feel powerless. I figured if he kept yelling at me she was going to get one of his guns and shoot him. I'd read that was how most all violent deaths occurred—by some pissed-off family member. I didn't want Angie to get locked up in a nuthouse or a jail. And even though I hated my dad at that moment I didn't think I could handle seeing him laying dead in front of me. So I said, "It's my fault."

I guessed my parents liked to trick us because maybe that made them feel like they were being pals. Like the morning after me and Laura were supposed to meet. My mom had finally said, "Well, there was a little rapping on your windowsill last night. I was half scared to death. I thought it was a burglar. Fortunately for you two girls I didn't wake your father."

"Who was it?" I asked nervously.

"I guess Laurie had decided she wanted to sneak out. She said she wanted to see if you wanted to go with her."

I breathed a sigh of relief. "Oh," I answered, not taking my eyes away from my mom, "what did you do?".

"I drove her home. It was after midnight. I didn't want her walking the streets by herself. Scares me to death imagining the little rat running over here all by herself at that hour."

"Did you tell her parents?"

"No. She got back in her house as quietly as she got out."

I knew when I saw Laura at school that day she'd go on about how cool my mom had been to her. But she didn't realize that she definitely had the better deal. Even if my mom had told Laura's parents she wouldn't have gotten in trouble. Her parents would just have said I was a bad influence. But if the opposite had happened and her parents had brought me home after midnight, I'd have been murdered. My parents would have accused me and said it was all my fault.

LAURA'S MOTHER AND father were sort of famous in Springfield. Her father was a college professor and her mother was a political activist. There weren't very many of those in our town. Mrs. Campbell was always on the news for leading an antiwar protest, an abortion-rights protest or a ban-the-bomb protest somewhere in the area. I would see clips of her holding a banner and shouting slogans into the cameras, or giving a speech or sometimes even scuffling with a cop.

My dad thought Mrs. Campbell was crazy and my mom, like most all the other middle-aged women around, admired her. The kids at school, me included, were mystified by Mrs. Campbell. She didn't wear makeup or dresses or have a salon haircut. And she would fight openly with anyone she disagreed with. In Thelma and Galena people fought in public all the time, it was half of the way they entertained themselves but in Springfield it was considered deviant behavior.

I had mixed feelings about Mrs. Campbell. I thought it was pretty cool what she did but I was afraid of her. Before I knew her I figured it was just because she was so outspoken.

Laura hated her mother. The first time I went over to their house, me and Laura had walked in the kitchen, where Mrs. Campbell was opening a can of Chef Boyardee ravioli.

"Is that dinner?" Laura sneered.

"Yes. You kids like the ravioli don't you?" Mrs. Campbell asked affectionately.

"No, us kids don't like the ravioli. We tell you that every time you open a can of it. Jeffrey even gets sick from it and you still fix the fuckin' shit."

"You know there are more effective ways to express yourself than cursing, Laura," Mrs. Campbell said patiently.

"What does it matter? You never pay attention to anything anyway," Laura said, opening the refrigerator. "Misty's mom cooks real dinners for them every night. Not this frozen and canned shit we have to starve on. And she even has a real job."

"How many children does your mom cook for, Misty?" Mrs. Campbell asked calmly.

"Me and my sister," I answered, feeling like somehow I was betraying Laura.

"Well Laura has six other brothers and sisters."

"That's no point. You shouldn't have had so many kids you can't take care of. Not that you'd be any different with one."

Laura's mom acted like she didn't hear her and said, "Laura forgets how difficult it is to cook for seven kids who all eat at different times."

"Yea," I said.

"Oh you're so full of shit. Quit talking to my friends about how rough your life is. You had the kids, no one asked you to. Why didn't you get some of those abortions you believe in so much?"

"Would you have wanted me to do that with you?"

"Anything would be better than this, I can tell you for sure. Instead my dad has to go out and abort his life to make enough money to feed us," Laura said, directing the part about her dad to me. "The least you can do is cook the crap. But she's too busy. Of course, she's not too busy to give you all the political reasons women have it so hard, how us girls really have to stick together. She says we're all so oppressed by the man's world. Like she ever did a day's work in the man's world to begin with."

I was beginning to feel anxious and I wanted to leave, but Laura kept yelling at her mother. "All these stupid college kids come around and listen to my mom's bullshit and think she's so together. Just shows what idiots college kids are. They'll listen to someone who can't make dinner, can't clean a house, can't keep her shit together, can't even earn a goddamn dollar, so we could have a decent allowance," Laura said as she slammed things around the refrigerator.

"Laura, someday you'll realize there are more important things in the world than money. Money is the least valuable," Mrs. Campbell said in a voice like a minister.

"Least important to you, but how would any of us survive if Dad wasn't around making the money, or your own mom and dad weren't sending us money to cover our asses? She gets an allowance from her parents and she's practically fifty and we can't even get money for the weekend from her. Why don't you get a real job so then maybe you could afford to hire someone to be our mother?"

"There are many people who don't have all that you have," Mrs. Campbell said as she plopped the contents of the can into a saucepan.

"Lucky them. My mom's real concerned about everyone else and their needs," Laura said as she grabbed two Cokes from the refrigerator and slammed the door shut. Then, with relief, I followed her out of the kitchen onto the back patio.

"Wow, I can't believe your mom lets you talk to her that way. My dad would have belted me fifty times for just complaining about dinner," I said, still nervous from the whole thing.

Laura shook up her Coke, then opened it up on an angle so that it sprayed all over the sliding glass doors. "She's on tranqs," Laura said matter-of-factly. "Usually we have to tiptoe around her so she won't freak out. But when she's on her headache pills we can take advantage of it."

As I got to know Laura better I found out her parents were as bad as mine, just in a different way.

I had always thought a big family would be great to have, but Laura told me it was worse. She said it just caused greater amounts of the same shit. Laura told me her dad had tried to leave her mom several times but every time he would she'd turn up pregnant again. She said he finally quit trying to leave to spare any more kids from having to be born into their situation. Laura said her mom told people it was her duty to have a lot of kids because we were becoming a small-family society. Her mom believed that made everyone more selfish and less concerned about the world. Laura said she believed her mom was insane because no one on the planet was more selfish than her mom, and the kids were so busy fending for themselves they never had time to think about anyone else's welfare. Laura also said her mom just had kids so she would have an excuse not to get arrested by the police if she made too much racket over some issue, she said she was too chicken to spend time in jail.

Knowing the way Laura felt about her mom made it impossible for me to look Mrs. Campbell in the face. I felt sorry for the shit Laura said her littlest brother and sister had to go through. Even though I had only seen Mrs. Campbell be real affectionate to the young kids it seemed like she was just holding on to them to keep someone from pushing her off the cliff she was on.

Laura had always said not to ever look at her mom anyway or she would ask you to do something for her. She said people had quit coming over to their house because every time they did her mother would try to get them to run to the store, or watch the kids, or carry some laundry, or pick up a prescription for her medicine. Laura said every now and then there would be a new neighbor or a young college kid on one of her mom's committees who got sucked in to being her friend but that soon enough, if they had any brains, they would realize the score and be gone.

Laura's mom was a scary woman. She was scary when she was calm from her pills because she was like a robot. And when she wasn't on them she was as spastic as a cat trying to run from a blue jay.

When I would tell my mom stories about Mrs. Campbell or tell her things Laura had told me she would say, "There's no way for us to know the whole story. I love Laurie but it's wrong for her to blame her mother so much. She didn't get pregnant by herself."

I was learning that women who had kids stuck together on everything. Because no matter what they didn't have in common with each other they shared one bond—they were misunderstood, taken for granted and abused by their kids and husbands. Their husbands, who were bound by the idea they had been trapped, nagged and forced to turn unromantic by their wives and kids.

But none of this stopped me from having visions of a perfect family of my own someday. I would have a husband who loved me and always wanted to kiss me. We would have a lot of happy kids we had fun with. We would eat all our meals together and talk about life and help each other when we didn't feel so good. I guess I still believed in the Waltons the same way I believed in Santa Claus, the Easter bunny and goblins. Years after everyone had proved to me they weren't real I still wanted to pretend they existed. The only problem was, any parents I had seen that were close to my picture of perfect always had kids who were boring and dull-witted. I ended up thinking, if I could find the kind of guy who was like the kind of guy who could be in jail, but wasn't in jail, or was ever going to be in jail—that would be the guy I would be able to have my perfect family with.

MY LAST YEAR OF high school was an easy time. My dad bought me my own car. It looked like a big pink box on wheels, but it was popular with all my friends because it could take on any terrain, it was crashproof and the front seats popped back to meet the rear one and form a bed.

After all these years my parents had begun to accept who I was, who Angie was, and who each other were and things seemed kind of calm around our house.

I had settled down too. I quit doing all drugs except pot and occasional mushrooms—and liquor wasn't considered a drug then. And I didn't care that much about boys because I was preparing myself for the whole world of new faces I would be meeting after my release. Freedom was finally in full view.

My senior year was the first year that I knew actual people, my own age, who died. Morris Latham had killed himself and left a note revealing a sordid other world he lived in. Mitchell Sinclair's body had been found stuffed in a dry-cleaning bag in the basement of an abandoned house. He had died of a drug overdose at a party and the kids who had been with him got scared and hid his body. The really gross part was that they put him inside a partially exposed brick wall and then tried to seal it up. As Mitchell's body decomposed it dripped and made the wall give way. He was discovered by the police after the neighbors had complained about a strong stench coming from the empty house.

Cherry Laughlin had gotten decapitated in a car wreck on the railroad tracks. Her boyfriend, Moss Brett, had lived and told everyone how he would never be the same person again after seeing Cherry's head laying away from her body. For quite a while after that he said he was going to be a priest.

And Melissa Shumacher hung herself in her father's office. Melissa Shumacher was one of the first girls I had ever known who said she would never get married and never wanted to have kids. She had said those things since junior high—a long time before anyone had heard it was a new way for girls to think. Melissa had known most things, though, before the rest of us. Her dad was a neurosurgeon and her mom was the daughter of a world-famous something in the brain department.

My mom told me that Melissa had probably been a frustrated genius and that was why she had committed suicide.

My sister Angie had dated Mitchell Sinclair for a short time. I was protective of Angie and I never wanted her to do the things I did or had done. When I found out she was doing drugs and having sex I threatened to tell my parents. When she was with guys I didn't approve of I would try and make her break up with them. When I found out that Angie was going out with Mitchell I did everything I could to get her to stop.

Mitchell was really handsome. He had longer hair than any other guy at school and looked like he was nineteen or twenty. He moved to our school in the middle of the year. It was rumored he had been kicked out of his last school but no one knew why. Mitchell was normally the kind of guy I would have liked myself but he had something creepy about him. I think in a way it was like he already seemed dead.

When I asked Angie what she saw in Mitchell she said, "What's it to you?"

I was always curious about the way Angie's mind worked because it was so different from anyone else's I knew. Angie was the only person I knew who was mysterious, and I had deep admiration for this quality in her.

John Meisner, who was the cutest guy in our neighborhood, had loved Angie since she was thirteen. I had always been friends with John and I had a crush on him when I was fifteen. We would have long talks and he liked me a lot but he told me Angie was the girl he was waiting for. He was five years older than her and would say that by the time she was eighteen, it wouldn't be so big of a deal, their age difference. A lot of girls had a crush on John but he was very serious about Angie.

We were sitting on our front porch once while he was waiting for Angie to come home from school. I asked him why he liked her and didn't like me that way.

"Oh, you're great, Mist. You always make me laugh, the silly things you say. But I always know what you're thinking. Angie, you can never tell what's in her mind. Most girls think they've got to talk all the time. Angie doesn't. She's just what girls are supposed to be. And those eyes of hers, big and dark and full of fury."

I thought he didn't seem that old now listening to him sound so lovesick over a girl who was only thirteen. But I wondered why all guys seemed to like Angie for the same reason. I figured if being mysterious and quiet was what it took to make the opposite sex fall in love with you, then I didn't have a hope in the world.

Angie didn't like John. She thought he was dull and boring. Every time she'd see him hanging around she'd leave. I thought it was unfair that he thought Angie was fascinating because she didn't talk to him. When the reason she didn't talk to him was because she didn't like him. And it seemed unfair that he thought I was obvious because I talked too much, when the reason I talked to him was so he wouldn't feel like a dope hanging around waiting for Angie to avoid him.

When Angie was little she never wanted anyone to feel bad. People were always saying about her, "What a precious child," "What a perfect angel," "If only they all were this sweet." She was the ideal of what a little girl is. She was beautiful, she laughed easy, she was gentle and giving and sweet. She hadn't gone through a demanding stage—grabbing things from other kids or trying to keep her toys or candy to herself. Anything Angie had she would share. And she never said mean things or teased other kids and was especially nice to the kids who were teased by others. But instead of being rewarded for being so nice and generous and easy, she felt she had been taken advantage of.

I had always taken advantage of Angie and I figured it was a lot my fault she had changed so much. She probably just got sick of being nice to someone who was only going to call her fat or stupid. I used to call her fat because she was more developed than me and it made me jealous boys liked Angie so much. Even before she had an Italian sex-symbol body, boys liked her better than they liked other girls.

By the time Angie was a teenager she had quit caring how anyone felt and had become a loner and a rebel. Not just someone who rebelled against authority and dumb rules and boredom but someone who was rebelling against the image everyone else had created of her. She was like my mom in this way. I asked my mom if, since she and Angie were so much alike, she loved her more than me and she said, "You never love one of your children more than the other one, but maybe you do love them in different ways for different reasons, because they're two different people. It's true Angie is more like me. She's not comfortable with her place in the world. People tell her she isn't the person she knows deep down she is. That's confusing. She had to walk in your shadow, to be compared, it's hard being the youngest, being called Misty Groves' little sister instead of by your own name. Angie doesn't know how much she's loved and I know what that feels like. Angie is my baby, the one I have to take care of.

"But you're my firstborn, my pride and joy. That makes you special in my heart a way nothing else can be. I admire you, I think you're brave and strong and lucky. I have high hopes for you, Misty."

I didn't believe my mom felt that way, because I always knew Angie was the strongest and the bravest. Angie wasn't afraid to get shots. I was the one who was afraid to sleep alone after I had watched a scary show. I was the one who couldn't walk down in the basement by myself or be alone in the woods or swim far out in the lake. Angie wasn't afraid to be in the house by herself, or walk in the dark or do dare-devil stunts. My mom would tell me, "Misty, you'll always get along great in the world because people embrace you, you fit in. Angie is an outsider, like me."

My mom didn't know me at all. First she thought I was brave and strong and then she didn't even know that I had felt outside of everything my whole life.

So I thought this was only my mom's way to tell me she didn't love me. Because she didn't really like people who were brave or strong. She'd always said she was partial to underdogs. I had thought that maybe like my mom Angie had the same notion about underdogs. Mitchell Sinclair was definitely that.

The more I tried to get Angie to tell me about Mitchell, the more she resisted. She had become resentful of any interference I had in her life and had started to treat me the same as I did Mom and Dad. Finally in a hateful tone of voice, Angie answered me, "You would never understand so don't ask."

"Try me," I dared.

"Why, you'll just call me stupid," Angie said.

"No I won't, I promise," I assured her.

"You always say that."

"But I won't, I swear to God."

"Why do you want to know?" she asked.

"Because I can't understand why you like him," I said.

"Well it's not your business really."

"It is too, I'm your sister."

"So?"

"So, that means I have a right to know."

"Well it doesn't mean that," Angie said.

"Just tell me, please," I begged. "I really want to know."

Angie glared at me for a few seconds, then said coldly, "Because he doesn't talk. I don't even like him that much. He just doesn't bug me. That's why I hang around with him."

"But he's dangerous."

"He isn't to me," Angie answered.

I couldn't understand what it was like to want to be around someone because they didn't talk to you. It was the exact opposite for me. But that was how Angie was. When Mitchell had been found dead I asked Angie if she felt bad and she said no because he had known he was going to die soon and that that was what he wanted and that, besides, she hadn't seen him for three months anyway.

Even the day we heard about Mitchell on the news Angie didn't cry. I couldn't get how it seemed so easy for her to act like she didn't care about things. I knew if I had gone out with a guy who died—even if I had quit liking him—I wouldn't be able to stop crying for a couple of years.

My mom had told me that when Angie was three weeks old she had rushed her to the doctor. My mom always laughed when she told the story. "I ran into his office hysterical and I said, 'I know I should've come sooner but I kept thinking it would change. She makes sounds, she cooes, but my baby doesn't cry.' The doctor asked"— then my mom would change her voice to sound deep and husky—" 'Well, has she ever cried?' " Then she'd change it to sound like an excited young woman. " 'When she was born. She cried once when the milk in the bottle was too hot and she cried when I accidentally poked her with a safety pin while I was doing her diaper.' I was crying myself by this time. And I was afraid the doctor would think I was an unfit mother. 'Well she sounds pretty normal to me. She cries when poked with pins. But let's take a look at her,' " my mom said, imitating the doctor again. "Then he examined her top to bottom and said, 'She's in A-one shape. It happens that some babies just aren't criers. Consider yourself one lucky little lady, most young mothers would kill for your problem.' "

The last time I had seen Angie cry was in the seventh grade, when she fell out of a tree. I had yelled for my mom and dad as soon as I saw Angie fall from the tree. My mom and dad ran outside as Angie screamed, "My leg!" She was writhing on the grass in our front lawn.

"Quit acting like a baby. I know a broken leg when I see one and that's not a broken leg. Get up and walk, move around on it. You'll be OK," my dad ordered as he forced her to get up. But as soon as she stood Angie yelled out in pain and fell back down.

My mom was pleading with my dad, "Will, I think she's hurt. Let me take her to the hospital."

"I'm not paying any goddamn doctor bills for a bruise. Maybe it'll teach her to stay out of that tree."

Angie's face was white and pasty as she lay on the ground. I had tears in my eyes because I could see how much she was hurting. My mom bent down to put her hands on Angie's face. "She's cold. I'm taking her to the hospital."

"Get back in the house," my dad ordered. "You're hysterical. It was a little fall."

"I'm not hysterical. You either help me get her in the car or I'll do it myself. And if you try and stop me, so help me God, you'll regret it," my mom said threateningly.

"I'm not paying for it," my dad argued.

"I've worked every day of my life. I've more than supported this family on my salary. You can keep your goddamn money, you selfish bastard." Then my mom told me to go in the house and get her purse and keys.

When I ran back outside and helped my mom carry Angie to the car my dad shook his head and said, "Fools. You're all fools."

At the hospital the doctors told my mom that Angie's leg was broken in four places and some of the bones in her foot were smashed. They said it looked like she had tried to walk on her leg and that had caused the damage to be more severe.

Angie had to wear a full leg cast for nine months, the whole part of her seventh-grade year. My dad had never said he was sorry for not believing her and had only gone once to visit her in the hospital.

Angie changed a lot after that year. It was weird how so many things I could look back on in our family as a moment when something changed, never to be the same again. And it was weird to me how I could have so many horrible pictures of my dad in my head, followed immediately by a tender memory.

I remembered the night him and my mom had a big fight and were saying they were going to get a divorce. I had done my usual sobbing and begging them to stop. Then my dad lifted me up and carried me outside. He took me into the backyard and sat me on top of one of the doghouses so we'd be face to face. I was in my pajamas and it was freezing cold out. My dad took off his shirt and wrapped it around me. I was still crying as I pleaded, "Please don't get a divorce. Please don't leave us. Please, Dad."

"I won't ever leave you. Wherever I went I'd take you with me," he said, wiping the tears from my face.

"But we can't leave Mom and Angie alone. They would die without us. We can't leave," I cried.

My dad held me close to him, tight, to stop me from shivering. "You're too young to get yourself so worked up, baby. These are grown-up things you can't understand. Everything will be all right. I won't ever leave you. I promise. I'll always love you more than anything, Misty. I always have, I always will," he whispered as he carried me back inside.

And I had always believed him. Even when I knew I couldn't anymore.

So things were a lot different for us now that I was seventeen. But it seemed like Angie was the most different of all.

I PROBABLY SHOULD'VE been born the youngest child in a family with lots of big brothers. I believe if this had happened I wouldn't have had so many boyfriends. For me, the search for brotherly platonic love was as deep and elusive as the search for romantic love. But I could never tell which one I was looking for, or when or who I was looking for which one with. The only thing I did know for sure was that I could never have sex with someone who was my friend and I couldn't be friends with someone I was having sex with. Which was kind of a drag, because by the point I knew a boyfriend long enough to be his friend I could barely even kiss him. But I would still be faithful.

The only time I've ever been unfaithful to one of my own boyfriends was towards the very end of our relationship, or when they were really mean to me, or when I simply couldn't avoid it because of extenuating circumstances.

I try very hard to avoid circumstances which are extenuating. When I have a boyfriend I become a real homebody. If I do go out to a party or a dinner or the store, I don't flirt. Even when guys try to flirt with me I won't flirt back. To me flirting is just liking someone sexually and I only sexually like a person I know I'm going to have sex with. I can honestly say I never, hardly ever, flirt. I don't buy what all the magazines and advice columns tell you—that it makes you feel pretty and it's good for your ego and that it's healthy. Besides, the one time I did flirt I ended up having sex with my boyfriend's best friend, who happened to be my best friend's boyfriend. I would've married him, though. As a matter of fact Jack

O'Hara was the only guy I had ever met who I would have married. It was because I felt that way that I rationalized why I had betrayed my best friend.

I had been in love with Jack O'Hara from the moment I saw him. Jack was sitting on the railing of his front porch rolling a joint. After he twisted the ends between his fingers he quickly slid the joint between his lips with just enough wetness to seal the paper. The very first thing he said to me was "Nice car." He said it like he was telling me, "You're what I like. Let's go be alone together for a week or two." Then he grinned the kind of way that made it look like we were sharing some inside thought together.

Jack had straight, soft, white hair that came to his shoulders and blue, blue eyes that I was too enraptured with to even be embarrassed by my car—which was old and clunky and pink.

I had driven over to Jack's house with my then boyfriend, Darryl Clement, who had just started hanging out with Jack. Darryl had tried to keep me from meeting Jack because he was afraid I'd fall in love with him. He didn't tell me that but I knew how jealous and paranoid Darryl was. He was always giving me the silent treatment or yelling out loud at me for talking or looking at another guy.

Me and Darryl had been together over a year by this time and I already knew I wasn't in love with him anymore. Darryl was the first guy I'd ever had an adult relationship with. I call it adult because I was seventeen and didn't live with my parents anymore, so Darryl was the first guy I ever got to wake up with in the mornings.

We met officially at a keg party my last week of high school. I had gone to parties, snuck in bars or been at rock concerts where Darryl was before and thought he was really cute, but I had never actually talked to him. He was always surrounded by people—girls mostly or his two best friends.

Darryl Clement, Kyle Cantwell and Mike Dodge, who was called Dodger, went everywhere together and were famous locally as a "stamp-of-a-good-time" seal of approval at events. I was excited as soon as I walked in the party and saw Kyle because I knew that meant Darryl was there too.

I told my friend Pam, who I had come to the party with, that I would be really depressed if I saw Darryl at the party with another girl. She passed me a beer and said, "School's out, it's over, you never have to get depressed again. The world is an open place, it's our oyster. If he's with someone else, fuck him," then she toasted my cup and whispered in my ear, "Celebrate."

It was a great party, everyone was happy. We talked about school, teachers we liked, ones we hated, classes we hated, with total abandon—not the way we said we hated something on a Friday night, knowing it was going to be right back in our face on Monday. I was feeling so good I didn't even want to see Darryl because it would interrupt my freedom. Right then was when Darryl walked over to me. Nothing had ever come to me in my life until I didn't care about it anymore. Darryl lifted the Styrofoam cup I was drinking from out of my hand. "You don't look like a keg head," he said. Then, like he was handing me a bouquet of roses he pulled a Heineken from behind his back. Heineken was a badge of coolness and wealth in our town because it was so hard to get.

I could tell right off that Darryl liked me but I couldn't understand why. He was older than me and lots of girls wanted to be with him because he grew the best pot, had lots of cash and drove a Volkswagen van. He also looked just like Leon Russell if Leon Russell took the silver out of his hair.

Darryl spent the rest of that evening paying attention to me. Every time I'd go over to talk to someone or get another beer he'd be waiting for me when I turned around. If we were across the room from each other he'd be staring at me or give me a wink. He made me nervous because I thought that any minute I'd say something that would make him turn and walk away, so I didn't say much of anything and kept trying to walk away from him instead. When I was getting ready to leave he grabbed my hand and pulled me into a hall closet. "I've got you alone in the dark now," he said. Then he kissed me.

I really like the way Darryl kissed—it made me feel like I should get out of the closet because if I didn't I would want to stay in it forever.

"I've gotta go. My ride's waiting for me," I said when I backed away from him.

"She'll wait. Can't you feel it? Time is standing still right now."

I started laughing and Darryl laughed, and I liked the way he laughed without making what he had said feel less romantic.

"Where did you get to be so pretty?" he asked.

"You're making me embarrassed." My stomach was beginning to feel tight and I didn't know how to answer him. I had never thought I was pretty but Pam had told me that you never tell a guy you don't like the way you look.

Darryl seemed so sure of what he was doing. He wasn't clumsy and begging the way most of the guys my own age were. But at least with those guys—since it really didn't matter what they thought—I didn't feel like such an idiot.

"I bet you got it from your mom," he answered.

"Got what?"

"Your pretty face."

"Everyone says I look like my dad."

Darryl started laughing and even though I hadn't tried to be funny I felt like I had said the right thing.

"Let's neck," he said pulling me up to him.

"I've really got to go. I can't see in here anyway."

"I want to keep you in the dark so you can't see how old I am."

"How old are you?"

"Twenty-two."

"Wow."

"I can buy your liquor for you."

"I have a fake ID. It says I'm twenty-one."

"You could carry me in your pocket instead of a fake ID. I'd hate to see you go to hell or jail for your criminal ways."

"Sure." I laughed. Still I logged it that Darryl could be a good liquor store contact if I ever needed one. We made out some more before I left the party with Pam.

Pam was my best friend for my last two years of high school. I had best friends the same way I had boyfriends. I had always had lots of friends who were guys but only one boyfriend at once. I always had lots of girlfriends but only one best friend at a time. We were loyal to each other, preferred each other over anyone else, and if we shared our secrets with another girl it would have been the same as cheating on a boyfriend.

When we got in the car Pam said, "Well I guess you don't have to be depressed. Kyle Cantwell told me Darryl was asking if you were going to be at the party tonight. He's in love with you." Then she made funny kissing noises and giggled, "You've graduated."

Two weeks after school was out I moved away from home. Darryl came over all the time. We had many nights of great sex and whole days where we talked about what our life together would be like and how much we loved each other.

Some people, though, couldn't understand how me and Darryl were together. Guys thought it was because I had some special sex secret and girls, especially the ones Darryl's age, thought he stayed with me because I was too young and dumb to hassle him about anything.

One night at a party a girl came over to me. I had seen her before but she had never acknowledged my existence. "Hi," she said. "You and Darryl have a thing, don't you? I've seen you around."

"Yea," I answered.

"He sure is cute. I guess that's how he gets all his girls. Blond girls, that is, he only goes for blondes. You know his last girlfriend had a nervous breakdown when he left her. She didn't eat and wouldn't leave her apartment for five days. Her brother had to bust the door in."

Lots of people had felt obligated in the past to warn me of Darryl's reputation as a heartbreaker but none of them before had tried to make me feel like I deserved it if it happened.

"Anyway I thought you oughta know. He'll really hurt you," she added with a twisted grin.

The girl's voice was craggy and her breath smelled like the top of a sticky bar counter. Her face looked like something was pulling her expressions away from her. It was obvious she couldn't hold her liquor.

I didn't want to be angry with her, but she was too old to be reformed by forgiveness, so in a cold, definite voice I said, "Well thanks for the advice but I'm not too worried about it."

I wasn't so mystified as everyone else seemed to be as

to how Darryl was with me. I knew he loved me. I knew it from the way he looked in my face, from the things he said to me and from the way he always wanted me with him. I knew so much that Darryl loved me I was never even jealous. This was the only time in my adult life this phenomenon occurred. And I blame Darryl for my slightly extreme problem with jealousy in later years. He brainwashed me to think it was a sign of love and would say I didn't care about him since I wasn't jealous. I thought it was because I trusted him and that that was the way it was supposed to be. But I was too young then to know that I was right.

When I fell out of love with Darryl it seemed to happen as quickly as when I fell in love with him. It had taken me one night in a closet to promise myself to him forever and one afternoon in a canoe to know I'd never like him again.

One Sunday Darryl came over to my apartment and asked me to go to the lake with him to try out his new boat. I said, "Aren't you supposed to take a canoe on the river?" This made Darryl mad. He hated it if I ever acted like he was making a mistake. In an impatient voice he explained that he wanted to try it out on still water at Larkspur Lake.

Larkspur Lake was more like a gigantic pond. It was a really corny place and hardly anyone ever went there unless they were really young, or really old, or couldn't

afford the gas to get to better lakes farther away. Still, I
didn't mind going to Larkspur because I figured that
meant it would be a short day.

When we got to the lake Darryl unloaded the canoe.
It took him a while to undo the knots he had tied and
the whole time he complained that he was damaging his
fingers. Darryl had sensitive fingers, he claimed he didn't
have as many bones in them as he was supposed to, and
that his hands were always in pain and becoming deformed because of it. But Darryl had lots of ailments. If
he didn't have an ailment he'd damage some body part
in an accident and if he couldn't find anything physical
to whine about he'd have something wrong with his van
or stereo or some other material object.

After Darryl shoved us off from the shore he realized
he had forgotten the oars. Larkspur had a mud bottom,
not gravel like most other lakes. I watched Darryl trudge
through the shallow water and up the bank to his van,
his jeans soggy with mud. He was shaking his hands so
that I could see they were in pain again. I was curious if
I would've fallen in love with Darryl if he was doing this
on our first day out together. I thought about all the girls
who would say to me, "God, you have got the coolest
boyfriend," and I wished I could've pulled any one of
them out of the air and given them my seat.

By the time he got back to the boat I was in too bad
of a mood to even be laughing. Which was just as well,
because Darryl was even more sensitive to being laughed
at then he was to injuries.

We rowed around for a while. The day was perfect—crisp and sunny and filled with the smell of crushed fallen leaves—and pretty soon I was enjoying myself. We drank some beers, then got romantic. Darryl stopped rowing when we got to a part of the lake that was surrounded by tall wooded cliffs. We balanced in the canoe, then I wrapped myself around him as he sat on the middle bench and we had sex. As I put my shirt back on I looked up and saw a house built into the side of the hill. A man was standing on the balcony looking through binoculars. I felt embarrassed and mad at Darryl and immediately flashed back to the time my dad caught me and Darryl in bed together.

One morning, not long after I moved out of my parents' house, my dad came over to take me for a ride on his motorcycle. The front door was unlocked, so my dad had walked in the house when I hadn't answered his knock. We heard him call my name out just before me and Darryl saw him standing in the doorway of my bedroom.

My room had two doors, the one my dad was at and a set of French doors that opened onto the backyard patio. Darryl had jumped out of my bed when he heard my dad's voice. As soon as he saw my dad looking at him he threw open the French doors and without even grabbing his clothes he took off running, completely naked, across the back lawn. I watched him clumsily jump the hedges. Behind the hedges was a 7-Eleven, a big parking lot and a busy intersection—and no place for an undressed person to go.

I grabbed the robe that was thrown across my bed and ran to my dad, who was already walking away. All I could see was his face—the way it looked as he walked in my room. The second it took my dad to see what he was seeing turned his face from one of the excitement he had anticipated in surprising me with his new motorcycle to the horror of a person discovering some brutal, bloody murder scene. He so much didn't want to believe what he was seeing, his expression jumped back. Then he knew it was true and everything fell. I had just watched my dad die and I was in shock, not knowing what to do or who to call.

"Dad, Dad, wait," I yelled out.

He was already starting his motorcycle by the time I caught up with him. I stood in front of his bike, thinking he wouldn't run me down. All I could get out of my mouth was "Please." Stuff was running down my leg from standing up so soon, it felt warm and thick and slow. My dad said, "Give me the keys to my house."

"Don't do this," I pleaded.

"Give me my keys."

"Dad, please talk to me." I wanted to yell at him, to scream, "What's the big deal? You've been accusing me of this since I was thirteen. Why are you having a heart attack over it now? You always thought this about me!" I felt like grabbing him, crying and begging him not to leave, but I knew he wouldn't talk to me anymore and I didn't want to take a chance on him noticing what was dripping down my legs.

My dad left without even looking back and if I hadn't moved from in front of his motorcycle I'm pretty sure he would have run me down. It was five months before he would talk to me again and ever after that he made me call him by his first name.

Darryl had avoided my dad since that day. He hadn't tried to talk to him or tell him he really loved me or that I wasn't a bad person. If he knew my dad was coming over to my house he'd leave, if I was at my parents' house he wouldn't come over. As I watched him smirk about the man on the hill and stand up in the boat to zip up his pants, all I could think about Darryl was what a pussy.

"I want to go now," I said out loud.

Darryl was in a giddy mood from knowing the man had seen us have sex. He was acting drunk. "Oh come on over here. Think what you're doing for the old man, seeing a sweet young thing like you."

"I want to get out of here," I said, moving to the other bench.

"Listen, don't get all bent out of shape, just 'cause some geezer that'll never see you again has a set of binoculars."

"Is this the kind of thing that turns you on or some-thing?" I asked. But Darryl was so out of it still he thought I was feeling good and trying to be funny.

"You're the kind of thing that turns me on. C'mere."

I could see now it wasn't that Darryl wanted to be with

me so much, he just wanted other people to know he could be.

"You're a true perv."

Darryl laughed. He was so dense he thought I believed he was cute.

"Where did you go that day my dad came over to my house?" I asked. I had never said anything to him about that morning, never told him how much he had let me down.

"What're you talking about?"

"The day my dad caught us in bed. Where'd you go? You were naked."

"I hid on the other side of the bushes and ran back in for my clothes when you went out front with your dad." He laughed again.

"Why didn't you wait then until I came back in?"

"Because I didn't know if you'd be back in alone."

"You didn't come back for two days."

"Look, your dad would've killed me if he'd seen me anywhere near you." Darryl was still laughing. He had probably laughed about how he'd cut out on me a hundred times before with his friends.

"My dad wouldn't have touched you. But you didn't even care enough to see if I was OK. You never asked me about it. And you never said anything to my dad."

"Like what would I have said, genius?"

"Like I wasn't a slut or something. Like that you loved me and had told me that. You didn't have to leave me there by myself."

"Well he's your dad." Darryl started paddling the boat into the marshes ahead of us.

"Let's hang out here awhile. I want to smoke a joint."

"You'll hide in here to smoke a joint and you wouldn't do it to have sex?"

"Look, I didn't hear you complaining."

I hated Darryl. But just for a minute, then all the anger and hatred I felt for him passed away. I thought about the times he had accused me of flirting and been rude to my girlfriends because he thought they were going to lead me astray. I thought about the time he had laid in bed all day and smoked pot because he couldn't think of anything else to do. I thought about the fact that his dream for the future was to own a crawfish farm. And I thought about the way he was always shaking his stupid fingers while mumbling, "Crippled," just loud enough to be heard. I felt nothing for Darryl.

Finally he said, "Let's get out of here as long as you're going to be such a sour ass." Darryl started to oar but the boat wouldn't move. We were stuck in the glades. "Shit, goddamn it," he yelled. He got out of the boat to push and pull the canoe into the water again. I started laughing and he threatened to turn the boat over if I didn't shut up. But instead of scaring me it only made me see what a fool he was. Darryl screamed and cussed and cried about the prickles from the reeds the whole time. When he got back in the boat he started pointing out and counting all the scratches and red marks he had on him.

When we got to the van Darryl couldn't get the canoe

tied back to the top. While he was kicking the van and the fenders and beating on the boat I asked, "How'd you get it on earlier?"

"I don't need your wise-ass bullshit. Shut up and get in the car," he screamed, slamming his finger into the tip of the canoe as he got it on top of the van. Darryl jumped up in pain, hitting his head on the same place he'd hurt his hand, and knocked the canoe off the van. Cuss words poured out of his mouth and tears were welled up in his eyes, he was jumping around on the bank, kicking the gravel and whipping his hand up and down. He looked like a war dancer gone loco from too much peyote.

I felt like I was going to burst from holding all my laughter in. I wanted to laugh, not just from how absurd he looked but from the relief of knowing this was the last time I'd ever be able to believe Darryl Clement was a cool guy again. I could finally walk away from him without thinking I was making a mistake and losing the best boyfriend I might ever be able to get. I finally felt sure of all the things I'd been uncertain of for the last year.

Darryl stopped jumping and looked at me to see what I was doing. I think he was hoping I would be laughing so he could freak out on me.

"You better get in the fucking van," he said. I would've laughed in his face right then, but I knew he'd hit me or kick me or kill me. Then he turned his back to me and started walking toward the water. I was hoping he was walking to the water to drown himself.

It took Darryl another hour to load the canoe, but at least he didn't make another sound the whole time.

I broke up with Darryl that day but he didn't know because I was too afraid to tell him. We went out for a couple of months after that until I made myself so unbearable to him he finally told me it was over. I acted all upset, I even believed I was upset, that I was heartbroken, that I would never recover. I cried, I thought I would die, I begged him not to go. I told him I loved him. I didn't know why I did all this at the time. Because I believe the truth was I hadn't wanted to be with him really since the day I watched him run naked out of my house. Or maybe it was since the day I first saw Jack O'Hara sitting on his front porch.

THINGS HAD CHANGED for me quite a bit since that time. I was living back at my parents' house. I knew I had never been in love with Darryl Clement. I had a different car and I had a new best friend, Loretta Lindsy—who only by coincidence was Jack's girlfriend. They said they were boyfriend and girlfriend, that is, but they both were fooling around on each other a lot.

Loretta was the wildest girl I had ever met. Not just wild in the way of doing drugs or having lots of sex.

Most everyone I knew did that, though it seemed like they did it because they were bored or didn't want people to think they were chicken. Loretta did everything she did because she wanted to, she didn't care what anyone thought about her, she was completely unafraid.

Loretta was beautiful like a little kid is, like a little boy. She had short blond hair and always wore tight, worn jeans and tight flannel shirts unbuttoned to where you could see what she wanted you to see. Loretta lived with her parents on a huge cattle ranch just outside of town, and her dad was a millionaire.

Before I actually met Loretta I had described her to my mom and my mom had said, "All millionaires have wild kids. That's because all millionaires have maids and nannies. Maids and nannies don't yell at the kids because they're afraid they'll lose their jobs and the parents don't have any reason to yell at their kids because someone else is doing their job for them. I've taught plenty of rich kids and they're all alike, every one of them. Wild, don't care what you think, know they can get away with the world."

My mom believed being a schoolteacher had enlightened her to the ways of all kids and their parents. She also believed it was the source of her bitterness.

Every day my mom said she hated her job and didn't like kids but she was the favorite teacher at her school. Kids always were glad when they found out they'd been assigned to her class. Partly it was because she was younger and prettier than all the other teachers but it was also because she spent more time trying to do it well than any of the other teachers.

My mom was famous at her school for having the most beautiful bulletin boards and holiday decorations and all the other classrooms would visit her class to see them. Once she made a bulletin board with the kids' school pictures. It had a 3-D pirate's chest and shiny, hard gold foil cut into coin shapes. She had cut out round photos of all her students and glued them to fit in the centers. Then she stuck the picture coins on the board so they looked like they were flowing out of the pirate's chest. In the same gold foil she cut letters and spelled out MY TREASURES ARE GOLDEN.

I would go wait for my mom after school sometimes just to stare at that board. The pictures of the smiling kids and the gold borders as shiny as a mirror made it seem as rich and desirable as any sunken chest you'd want to find. It made the kids really look like something valuable.

Loretta and me got together the same way I'd gotten with most of my boyfriends—we got drunk together at a party, stayed up all night talking and joking around, and started hanging out ever after that. The night we met at the party we sat on a couch, drank margaritas and tuned out all the activity around us. Every once in a while someone would come over and try to talk to us but we'd just ignore them. Not to be rude, we just didn't have time for them. We talked about boys first and even though we had the same history with them we'd approached it all very differently. Loretta was with guys because they made her feel good and I was beginning to believe I was with them just so I wouldn't have to feel anything.

Loretta started pointing out all the guys at the party she had slept with and we had even been with most of the same ones. We couldn't decide if it was because we had so much in common or just lived in too small of a town.

"Do you know Stanly Raider?" I asked.

"Oh yea," she drawled.

"He's cute but he's got a problem."

"I know just what you mean." Loretta giggled.

"After he got married he would still try to get me to do it with him. Like I would even if he wasn't someone's husband."

"He does that to everyone he slept with before him and Sheri. He's trying to prove to us all that he learned something," Loretta said with a wink.

"Ohhh. You're right I bet," I answered. I thought Loretta was really smart because I never would have figured that out on my own.

Loretta was the first girl I had felt like I could really talk to since Pam had moved away from town. And like most people who have lost a loved one, I spent some of that night reminiscing about Pam with Loretta.

"I miss her a lot. You would've really loved her. We met in gym class. Pam had just moved here from Colorado, but she had lived all over the place, all over the world. Japan, India. How does anyone who's ever been to India find Springfield?"

"They don't find Springfield, they lose India," Loretta said. We started laughing so hard we were falling into each other, trying to prop the other one against the back of the couch. We were really drunk. "See that guy? Joe Smith?" Loretta pointed out.

"Yea," I answered curiously.

"He's foreign. You know what they say about foreign men." She laughed.

"Yea right. Joe Smith? What is he?"

"Dangerous. He's got Russian hands and Roman fingers."

"My mom always says that. Only she thinks they're Roman hands and Russian fingers," I said. I was laughing so much I felt like I was being tickled.

"Mine too." Loretta sounded like she was swallowing her words from not being able to stop laughing.

"We're getting old." We sighed together. We took deep, deliberate breaths and tried to calm down but every time we would look at each other we'd burst out laughing again and say, "Ahh. Foreign men."

Finally we were sitting still, just kind of recuperating. "What were we talking about?" I asked.

"Before we lost it you mean?"

"Yea. Where was I? I was going to tell you . . ."

"We were talking about boys," Loretta said, trying to lead me back to what I'd forgotten.

"Nooo," I answered, trying to think, using everything we said as a clue. "It was something important."

"Hmmm." Loretta pondered.

"Pam! Oh yea, Pam. How we met."

"Oh yea," Loretta answered attentively. We were fully recovered from our fit.

"Mrs. Bush was making us play softball and me and Pam were on the same team and she just walked over and started talking to me. Know what she said?"

"Yea."

"You do?"

"No."

"She said, 'These gym suits are worse than the ones from my old school.' " Me and Loretta started laughing again. I was slapping her thigh and rubbing tears from my eyes. "Then she said, 'Only a gym teacher could invent an outfit that showed so much skin and is still this unsexy.' " We couldn't catch our breath we were laughing so hard. "You had to know Mrs. Bush to really appreciate this. She looked like a fat, ol', ugly man. And she hated girls and boys hated her."

Barry Uless walked over and said, "Hey, I want whatever it is you girls are on." Loretta fingered him and he said, "Sociable, real sociable. Remind me to never invite you to one of my parties."

At the exact same time me and Loretta answered, "Remind us it's your party and we won't be there." We hadn't stopped laughing as Barry walked off.

As good as I felt with Loretta, though, talking about

Pam that little bit had made me remember how much I missed her.

Pam was the kind of girl everyone liked, and guys liked her a lot. She wasn't all that good-looking but she was distinctive and she had one of those deep, husky voices that were really rare in Springfield unless you were a fifty-year-old lush. Pam also had a high tolerance for drugs and liquor and guys were impressed with her endurance. Pam had gotten married when she was sixteen but the married part of her life didn't seem real to me because her husband hadn't ever lived in town. I'd met him a couple of times and gone to their wedding but I didn't really know him. His name was Darcy Wilcox but he called himself Cherokee and always wore a bandanna. He was Irish, with red hair and freckles, and I thought he was pretty weird for wanting to pass for an Indian. Once when I asked him what he did he said, "I'm a hitchhiker." I didn't say much to him after that.

Pam and Darcy had met in Colorado and he would come visit and stay at her house with her and her parents. Pam talked about Darcy a lot when he wasn't around but most of what she'd say was drug-related. She would say, "I talked to Darcy last night and he told me he'd eaten the purest acid and had this heavy, religious trip," or "Darcy called. He just got turned on to some real peyote," or "Darcy's bringing me back some Turkish hash."

When she told me they were getting married I asked her why and she said, "Because I can't live without him."

"Do you love him?"

"Yea and he needs me. It would kill him if I didn't marry him."

The only person I had ever known who I thought would die without me was my mother. Even though she was mad at me most of the time she was always begging me to never leave and saying she didn't know what would become of her if I ever moved away. I couldn't imagine it would feel any better hearing these things from a guy, even one you loved.

We were in Pam's bathroom that day. She was sitting cross-legged on the counter facing the mirror and curling her eyelashes. Pam considered herself a hippie but she wore tons of makeup and rolled her hair. She had a ritual with it. She'd take a shower, then blow-dry her hair, then roll it on hot curlers, then put on face cream, powder, blush, some kind of eye-concealer stuff that older women use, green eyeshadow, eyeliner and five coats of mascara on her lashes that had been curled for three minutes. This took her an hour and twenty minutes. She did it twice a day on Friday and Saturday.

Pam's mom was the only mother I knew who tried to get her daughter to wear more makeup. When she'd come in the bathroom where we were she'd say, "Don't you think Pam would be pretty if she wore a nice, bright red lipstick and some blue on her eyes instead of that green?"

I was close to Pam's parents, I spent a lot of time at their house and even if Pam wasn't home I'd hang around and talk to them but they were different. Boss, which is what her dad was called by everyone, had been in the

FBI and Helen had never worked a day in her life. She didn't even keep a clean house. It was neat but it wasn't clean like my mom kept our house. Pam was always envious of the way my mom made our house, but she wouldn't have thought it was so great if she'd had to listen to her gripe about it all the time the way I did. Of course, even though it was a drag to listen to my mom I guess it was kind of convenient not to have to wash the dishes before you ate out of them.

Helen was batty and even though I talked to her about some of my problems she didn't do much more than laugh or say things like "Well, at least he's cute," "Have another donut," or "If you started wearing lipstick you'd see a big change in your life."

Boss was retired and spent his days walking through the house looking for things to fix or reading books about how to make a hundred dollars into a million dollars. Pam got to do anything she wanted. She was also allowed to smoke cigarettes in her bedroom. She was allowed to have a job, go out every night and stay as late as she wanted and she didn't have to do any chores. She was always yelling at her mom for washing one of her shirts wrong or not folding her jeans with the crease down the front.

Sometimes Boss would get mad at Pam, if she stayed out all night or didn't go to school or wrecked their car. But Pam would just say, "I make my own money, you don't have a right to say anything to me."

Then Boss would stalk around the house for a while

and tell Pam she wasn't allowed to go out or use the car but wouldn't ever stick to it.

Pam was my best friend, we did almost everything together but I didn't understand her at all. I didn't know why she would rather have a job than go to school. It seemed to me like the only thing worse than teachers were bosses. I didn't know why she never wanted to stay home when she could do whatever she wanted right there and I couldn't understand why she didn't like her mom and dad. They were daffy in a way but as far as I knew all parents were, at least hers never bothered her. But I especially couldn't understand why she wanted to get married when she was only sixteen and there were so many guys left to meet in the world. It was like Pam had decided there was no future for her so everything was for the moment. She did a lot of drugs and drank a lot and had sex with different guys, even though she said she loved Darcy.

I knew that Helen wasn't against Pam getting married, she even encouraged it, like she thought being married might make Pam start wearing red lipstick and dresses. But Boss did not want it to happen. I remember the day he told me how he'd give anything to get her to change her mind. I was sitting on the floor leaning on her bathroom door, waiting for Pam to get home from work. Pam was the only person I knew whose parents had given her the master bedroom so she could have her own bathroom. Boss was sitting on Pam's bed, his fists at his sides pushing into the mattress, his head hanging over. He had tears as he said, "You know she's my baby girl and I don't want her to mess up her life. How do you tell someone they're making a mistake?"

I felt sorry for him but mostly I was thinking, You're someone's dad and you're asking a teenager how to keep your kid from getting married? I was uncomfortable with his emotion but decided I'd try to help him out. "Why don't you just tell her no? She's too young to do it without your permission."

"Because she'll only run away and go somewhere they'll marry her."

"No she won't, she'd have to go too far."

"I can't stand the thought of her leaving home or not knowing where she is. She will go away." Boss's voice was cracking.

"You can get the police after her," I said forcefully. I knew if Pam had been able to hear me it would sound like I was against her but mostly I was trying to let her dad know there were things he could do. And I also wanted him to stop crying.

"She'd just leave again," Boss answered.

"You can threaten to have her put in jail."

"She'd let me. You know how stubborn Pam is. She'd tell me she'd rather be in jail if she couldn't be married."

What a wimp he is, I thought. I couldn't believe he'd been in the FBI. "She wouldn't think that way for long. Not after she'd been in jail, especially if it's a bad one."

"It'd hurt me more than it would her to have her locked

up in a bad jail." Boss slumped further over. His voice sounded like there was no breath to push the words out of his mouth.

"Well use a good jail. It wouldn't be for that long—a lot shorter than her marriage will be," I said, trying very hard to sound patient.

I knew if I had told my dad I was getting married he would've said, "No way." There'd be no decision making about it. I couldn't even argue with him about not wanting to mow the lawn. But as much as I hated him for his strictness, at least he wasn't afraid of doing what he believed was right. Of course, the problem my dad had in believing he was right meant that everyone else was wrong.

Maybe I was being too hard on Pam's dad and he wasn't a wimp. Maybe he did have some doubt that being a grown-up didn't mean he knew all the answers. Maybe he really did believe Pam had to find out for herself that having a husband, a crummy house and a bunch of bills wasn't that much fun when you are sixteen. Maybe he was thinking that. But maybe not.

Loretta Lindsy had one of the biggest houses I had ever seen. It had four stories and was half a town block long. They had stables and Loretta had her own horse that she rode every day.

The first time I went over to her house was like meeting a guy you're in love with. I felt shy and unworthy. I couldn't even look around because I didn't want my feelings to be obvious.

When we walked in the house Loretta led me down a long, wide hallway into a kitchen that looked like it should be in a restaurant. Everything was oversized and chrome. Loretta opened the refrigerator to get us a soda and I saw food that I had only seen before in magazines or on TV. They had artichokes and avocados and bowls of noodles in shapes I didn't know existed. Instead of Welch's grape jelly there were fancy-shaped jars of orange or yellow or green marmalades. Sitting on the counter next to the refrigerator were four different kinds of bread, not sliced loaf bread, but round, black bread with sesame seeds on top, a loaf of bread shaped like a star and two skinny sticks of bread that looked like three-foot-long fingers. Sitting in a big ceramic bowl on the table we were at were some things the size of a softball with a hard, dark rosy shell. Loretta noticed me looking at them and said, "You like pomegranates?"

"I never had one." I had read about pomegranates in this child's collection of Greek mythology I had, but I didn't know what they were.

"They're not too great. A real pain in the ass to eat. But my mom keeps them around to impress people."

"Yea. My mom does that too. She uses wax peaches."

My mom had a thing about kitchens. She'd go over to people's houses and come home describing their kitchen like she was talking about a piece of cake. One day she had gone to visit Mrs. Mack, whose daughter had just enlisted in some branch of the armed forces. My mom thought Mrs. Mack had it made because she didn't have to work, her husband was out of town a lot and she was rich. But she never counted in that Mrs. Mack had a son who wanted to be a girl and a daughter who wanted to be a man, not any man but a Sergeant Carter, as in Gomer Pyle, type man. But maybe she would have paid that price to have a brick kitchen with yellow and green tiles.

My mom also liked bathrooms a lot. "Where's the bathroom?" I asked, figuring I'd give my mom a full report.

"Use the one upstairs, second door on the left."

When I walked in Loretta's bathroom the world became a bigger, more promising place to me. It was luxurious. It had a black tile floor, a black bathtub the size of my parents' big bathroom and there was a red marble counter that had three black sinks in it with ornate gold faucets and taps. There were eight monogrammed towels at least six feet long and as thick as a rug. A separate shower was in one end that had two shower heads on each wall, six altogether, and little seats were built in along two sides. My mom could've moved in to their bathroom and lived happily ever after. I wished I could invite her over to spend time in their bathroom. But it was possible that instead of making her happy it would've just made her more miserable about her own life. My mom had given up hoping she'd ever live in a place that was exactly what she wanted. She knew her and my dad would never be rich and if they were he wouldn't let her be extravagant anyway. It was just as well I couldn't bring her to see the Lindsys' bathroom. If I did it would only give her some reason to be mad at me or say I was calling her inadequate.

When I came back into the kitchen Loretta's dad was there. He was the only parent besides my own who I had met that didn't look like a parent. He was handsome—tall and lean, with salt-and-pepper hair, and even though he looked his age it was like he was the age he was born to be. Mr. Lindsy was wearing a sweat-stained cowboy hat, broken-in, blue lizard boots, dirty jeans and a silky, hot-pink cowboy shirt.

"Who's the newcomer?" her dad asked, taking off his hat and slapping it against his leg. He had a Mississippi drawl that made his voice sound just like Elvis Presley's. "You look like you could be some relation to Will Groves?"

"He's my dad," I answered. I felt uncomfortable knowing Mr. Lindsy knew my dad. People who knew him always felt strongly about him and usually it wasn't strongly positive. The people who admired him—mostly men and cocktail waitresses—thought he was clever, handsome, fun to be around and the greatest sportsman alive. But the other people—namely my mom's friends and my friends' parents—thought he was aimless, a carouser and a car wrecker. I didn't know if he was a carouser but he had wrecked most every car we'd ever owned.

From the time I was little anyone who did know my dad knew I was his kid. My mom told me this was the reason my dad loved me more than anyone else—since I looked just like him he could be certain I was his kid. My sister Angie was dark, like my mother, and had big eyes and full, pouting lips. My dad was always saying they had found her in a covered wagon surrounded by blood-thirsty hounds and taken her home to raise. We all used to laugh when he said this but I realized after a while that Angie didn't really think it was so funny.

Angie wasn't an orphan or a product of my mom's promiscuity. She looked exactly like what it would be to take my mom's face and lay it over my dad's face. It was just that I didn't look like my mom at all.

I think it was because of this I had tried so hard to be like her when I was a kid. I wore my hair short when she had short hair, I wore the same style of clothes she wore. I picked the same colors, the same movies, the same actors and actresses for my favorites as she would pick for hers.

Sometimes I'd be watching something with my mom on TV and I'd think, That lady is pretty. Then my mom would say, "That Debbie Reynolds just turns my stomach, how in the world did she ever get famous? Who could like her?" Then all of a sudden I'd find myself thinking, Ugh, I hate Debbie Reynolds. I did that with lots of things, even food. When I grew up I finally realized a lot of the things I felt were really only things I wanted to feel. I didn't like Heath Bars—they hurt my teeth. I thought Desi Arnaz was cute and Bobbie Gentry was pretty, and as handsome as my mom thought Pernell Roberts was, I thought he was gross. I guess I figured my mom would like me better if she thought I was just like her, since that seemed to be the thing that decided favorites in my family. But really, her and Angie were authentically matched. Even when I tried I could not fake liking divinity, but Angie and my mom could eat it forever.

They both loved hot peppers, which brought tears to my eyes if I even smelled them. And they both had quick tempers, were shy and very exotic-looking.

My dad called my mom "squaw" because she looked so much like an Indian. Guys used to whistle at my mom all the time and people would stop her on the street to tell her what a beautiful girl Angie was. They'd look over at me and say, "And you've got a fine son there too." When my dad's friends would meet my mom they'd say, "Will, you've got the most beautiful wife." They'd call her mysterious, and rare.

I wanted to be mysterious and exotic-looking too but nobody ever said that about me. My mom would say I was a girl-next-door type, an open book, that anyone could tell what I was thinking anytime. And that was true because I was always embarrassing myself by how easy I would blush or cry. I never cried on the playground when I was a kid—I wasn't that open—but during the story hours if the teacher read us a sad story, stuff like that, I'd cry over.

Loretta didn't look all that different from me. We were both blond and regular-sized, but she had managed to be exotic. Maybe it was because she rode horses or maybe it was because she had such a wild reputation and she would always say things like "I fucked him" or "I fucked that guy. What's his name, anyway?" without ever getting embarrassed. Or maybe it was because her dad was a millionaire.

"What's your ol' man up to these days?" Loretta's dad asked.

"Same thing as ever," I answered, hoping he'd go back outside. He was nice enough but I wasn't in the mood now to act like I had any interest in my dad or his activities. Just hearing about him only made me think about how bad we got along. It seemed like every time he looked at me he was criticizing me for something—the way I looked or laughed or said "yea" too much. He was always on me about what I was going to do with my life, like he had done so much with his, and he kept my mom and sister upset all the time. At least he wasn't around that much. He had never been around much, but used to I would miss him and worry about him, now every time he was gone I only hoped it would be for an extra day.

"Well tell him I said hello," Mr. Lindsy said, setting his hat back on his head. "You know we used to play pool together? He's a slick one."

"Yea, I know. Last night he won three cases of sweet gherkins."

"I guess by the time you're takin' a man's gherkins you've cleaned him out of everything else." Loretta's dad was laughing. He had the kind of laugh that had no apology in it, the laugh of a man with a lot of power over other men. I wanted to go home. Even though I hated it there, I didn't belong at this house. These people didn't worry about money, they didn't hate their jobs or care what their neighbors thought. They were happy. They had foreign foods in their refrigerator, they knew they could go wherever they wanted if they wanted to. They had big, fancy books on their coffee tables that they probably even looked at.

"Ret, tell your mom I'm heading over to Clinkers and will be back after supper. Nice meeting you, junior."

When he walked out the back door Loretta said, "What an asshole. He thinks we're all so stupid. Like we don't know he's going over to do Connie Staples."

"You're dad's having an affair?"

"Yea. With this slut that I used to let ride my horses. She's younger than my big sister even."

"Wow. Does he know you know?"

"He denies he knows I know. We don't talk here at this place about anything."

"God, my mom would kill my dad. They scream at each other over everything, over nothing."

"I think when I was a baby my parents used to do that, but they don't anymore. Now they just cohabit."

"What do you mean?"

"It's what my sister says. It means they don't talk."

201

"That sounds OK to me."

"It's not. I won't tell my mom what my dad said. And after supper she'll figure it out on her own, but she won't ask me if he said anything. Then she'll look through a magazine, take a pill and a drink into the bathtub and cry. If I see her I'll say, 'You OK, mom?' and she'll say, 'I'm fine. Just the steam from the bath.' She won't tell my dad he's a motherfucker, she won't hit him, she won't even tell him to stop fucking around on her. The most she'll do is ask if he's going to be home for dinner. And he'll always say yes because he's too much of a coward to watch her face get all sad if he says no. But he doesn't ever come home."

I couldn't imagine what it would be like to know your dad was having an affair. Sometimes I would wish I could catch my dad kissing some other woman so I could blackmail him into giving me a bigger allowance. But I didn't think he ever would kiss anyone else. Even though my mom was convinced he was a cheat, it was really her who wanted someone else. She would get crushes on the widow fathers of her students if they were rich or a little bit handsome. She had a terrible crush on Mr. Hewitt, the father of one of her straight-A kids. She described him as debonair because he was polite and wore suits or golf clothes. My mom was certain life with Mr. Hewitt would mean she'd always have a perfect, clean house, a perfect, quiet daughter and a perfect, thoughtful husband.

It was too bad she couldn't marry Loretta's dad, because even though he wasn't her type his house and his money were. She had passed the point where romance was important in her life. Not because she wasn't still young enough to enjoy it but she was too old to handle the heartbreak if it died. Which is probably why she tried to kill what romance there was left between her and my dad.

My mom had moved into my sister's old bedroom and taken over one of her twin beds. As soon as she would get home from school she would put on her bathrobe. If my dad was home my mom would go right to her bedroom. She'd get in bed and watch TV and read magazines and not cook dinner on those nights.

When I had come home that night and told my mom about Loretta's dad she said, "All men do that. As soon as they use you, squeeze out your youth, your love and your innocence they move on to untrodden ground. Of course it doesn't matter if they're the only man who hasn't trod on that particular ground—because who else but a whore and a traitor would be with a married man. But a man doesn't care as long as it's fresh turf for him."

AFTER I HAD SLEPT with Jack O'Hara I heard my mom's voice call me a whore and a traitor. I had felt really bad but for so long I had believed that Jack was the perfect guy, the one I wanted to marry, that I just did it.

Jack and Loretta had been together off and on since

before I knew either one of them. Some part of me believed that since I had met Jack before I had met Loretta, it was kind of OK to be more loyal to him and me than to me and Loretta. I had never heard Jack talk about Loretta and when she talked about Jack it was not romantic or about being in love. She also told me that they both slept around on each other a lot.

A week or so after I had slept with Jack, me and Loretta were driving out to her house. Loretta had been out of town for a horse show and was telling me about a cowboy she'd had sex with.

"He was hot, Misty. Lean and mean, just the way I like them," Loretta said.

"Does Jack know?" I asked.

"No, he'd kill me if he did."

"Why? You said he does it."

"Yea, but he doesn't know I do it," Loretta answered.

I wanted to tell her that he did know she was with other guys, but then I'd have to tell her how I knew. I knew because the night me and Jack were together he had told me he knew Loretta was with other guys all the time.

The night me and Jack had finally got together was a night we had seen each other at a party at Kenny Rochester's farm. Kenny Rochester was my first real boyfriend after Darryl Clement. I had a short interlude with Gene Sylvester but Kenny and me had stayed together for at least two of my birthdays, which was longer than I'd ever been with anyone yet.

By this time I couldn't say exactly when I met any of

my boyfriends or for exactly how long we'd stayed to-gether. At best I could recall what holidays I'd shared with them or which seasons we'd weathered together. I had developed the same relation to time as domestic an-imals. They know the difference between very long or very short whiles. Other than that, time is landmarked only by a change in routine, which, like house pets, I don't like at all.

I don't think I fell in love with Kenny at first sight. I was more intrigued by him than anything. He was in college and knew exactly what he was going to do when he got out. He wanted to be a diplomat. Everything he did was towards that goal. Kenny liked to have fun and get high but he never put it before his work. That was something I hadn't known in anyone. I thought Kenny had honor and nobility and was a genius.

Kenny expanded my universe. He talked about things in the world, not just who was having a party or who was getting laid or who had the best drugs. He could also talk about his feelings in a way that made them sound like something real you could touch. Always before, feel-ings had just seemed like a thing that swarmed around your head like hornets waiting to sting you.

Kenny had one of the most tragic pasts of any person I had known. Both his mom and dad were dead and he had two brothers who died. His mom had been in a skiing accident and gone into a coma and when his dad was flying to Colorado to get her, his plane crashed and he was killed. His mom stayed in the coma for six months, then had a miraculous recovery. Kenny said that when her and him and his brothers were all living together again it was the greatest, because his mom was so happy to be alive.

One day her and his brothers were out sailing on a lake. They had wanted Kenny to go but he wanted to be with a girl instead. That night when he got home his uncle was waiting for him and told him his mother and brothers were dead, killed by a drunk driving a speedboat.

But to meet Kenny no one would ever know his history. He laughed easier and was more hopeful than anyone I knew and that was why I loved him so much. Kenny had made me see the world had promise and that even though really bad things happened to you, life could still be a good place. He said he would always be sad about his family but he figured he was still luckier than most people because he had a really great family for a short while as opposed to a bad one for a long time.

I felt like I had known Kenny's parents from the way he described them. Kenny said his parents did some kind of work for farmers' rights because they thought the government was trying to exterminate the small farmer. But they didn't sound as if they were like Laura Campbell's mom—hysterical fanatics using the misery of the world as an excuse to avoid their own. Kenny said they talked about things like books and foreign places and politics. He said his mom and dad didn't fight and loved each other the whole married time they were alive. Kenny's parents seemed like exactly the kind of people I wanted to be, like they had the kind of family I wanted to have. I believed with Kenny it would be possible to have that for ourselves, together.

Me and Kenny moved in together officially a few months after we started going out. We had a real house with a fireplace and two bedrooms and a basement and a laundry chute. We fixed it up really nice and would cook dinners and have friends over and sometimes just be alone together and build a fire in the fireplace. And on Christmas we got a Christmas tree and decorated it together and drank eggnog. I hated eggnog but I figured that was what real families drank at Christmas.

I loved living with Kenny—for a while. Then we started to fight. I believed he didn't love me anymore because I got mad all the time and I got mad all the time because I didn't believe he loved me. I would get upset that he was never home enough and when he was he always had people around.

Kenny was a real social person and had lots of friends— guys and girls. At first this was one of the things I loved about him. Kenny didn't treat girls the same way other guys did, like they were OK to have for girlfriends but they weren't good enough for friends. I would tell my girlfriends how much I admired this about Kenny and they would ask, "But doesn't it make you nervous?"

"No. Because I trust Kenny more than anyone I've ever known. He's a flirt sometimes but who isn't? But he wouldn't ever lie to me," I'd say.

I felt proud to say this, to be able to feel this way. I

believed the reason Kenny was as friendly to girls as he was to guys was because he valued equality.

One time Loretta had said, "You know, Misty, I think Kenny is a great guy but do you always know what he's up to?"

"Yea. He tells me everything. He'll even admit when he's attracted to another girl. If he'd admit that he'd admit if he was sleeping with her," I answered, remembering all the times I had asked him if he liked another girl more than me. Kenny would tell me, "She's nice and pretty, but you're the one I want to live with."

I believed this meant he was brave and respected me enough to tell the truth. Most guys would just flat out tell you they didn't like another girl, or even make some mean joke about her. Kenny never said anything mean about anyone.

Loretta asked, "Are you guys faithful to each other?"

"Yea. I couldn't do it any other way. I'm not into messing around, I definitely couldn't handle it."

"Oh," she had said. Loretta sounded far off when she responded to me and I figured she was probably sad about the way her and Jack were always hurting each other without even knowing they were doing it.

One weekend Kenny and me had a big fight. I wanted him to drive to Thelma with me to visit my grandparents and he said he had too much homework. I got mad and started yelling at him. "You won't be doing homework. You'll just have your friends over and end up partying all day."

"Mis, I've got a huge test Monday. I've got to study. I'll go with you next weekend," he had said.

"No you won't. You'll get out of it then somehow too," I yelled back.

"I promise."

"You always promise and something always comes up."

"Well go by yourself then," he said, getting mad.

"I want you to go with me. You never go anywhere with me anymore."

"Well you're always bitchin' at me. Just go to your grandparents' and give it a break."

"I hate this. We fight all the time and all you ever do is tell me you have homework or have to see Doug or John or Jack. Everything is more important to you than me," I said, thinking about how even when we were together lately he seemed distant and distracted.

"I know it's hard for you to understand what it's like to have to work. Maybe if you did you wouldn't take it so personal when I have to," Kenny said.

Kenny always tried to make it sound like school was more work than a job. He was always telling me when I was off I was off but when he left class he still had tons of work to do.

"You always pull that. You think you're so superior because you're in college. I know what it's like to work. I go to a job. At least you're doing what you want. That makes it not even seem like work. You just always think

I'm stupid because I don't go to college like you and your high-IQ friends."

"I don't think you're stupid. Don't I always try to get you to go to school?"

"I've been in school, maybe it wasn't college but I know what it's like. It's like one long vacation," I said.

Kenny laughed. "Well it probably is the way you went to school."

I glared at Kenny, then said coldly, "I used to think you were the nicest person in the world. That you weren't one of those snobs who thought they were better than everyone else. But you're as bad as all those other people who think being in college or having some rich doctor parents makes them superior."

Me and Kenny both knew what things made each other mad by this point in our relationship and this was the one thing that upset him as much as he upset me by mentioning my job.

I had a dumb job. I worked in a music store that got about two customers a day if I was lucky. The music store was in a huge old building, in a part of town people had quit shopping in around 1962. Everything about it was old—my boss, the owner, the sheet music, pianos all had been there for years. And everything had dust on it, even though I had to dust all the time so the boss would be able to feel like he was paying me for something. I couldn't see how they stayed in business and I was especially confused as to why they had me working there when easily the boss could handle all there was to do himself.

My boss, Mr. Rosin, was an older guy who really wanted to come off like some kind of a father figure to me. He was constantly telling me how to run my life. I'd talk to him because it was kind of hard to avoid, being in a big empty store for eight hours with one other guy. So I'd let him advise me on things about my life, but his advice was pretty boring.

Once for Kenny's birthday I bought him an expensive guitar at the store because I could get a discount. Mr. Rosin had made "tsking" sounds as I gave him my money and my that-week's paycheck. "You should never buy such a costly gift for someone you've known so little time," he said, sadly shaking his head.

He was always talking this way, telling you to not ever do something, then taking a long pause to wait for you to ask why. I knew now, though, that even if you didn't ask why he would tell you anyway.

To be nice and to speed things up, I asked, "Why not?"

"Because you don't know how long these things will last, if they don't last you won't want to have wasted your money, and if they do last it gets very expensive topping the next year's gift. Starting out with this guitar, if you stay together, by the time you are thirty you will have to buy him a house."

"Yea, well I don't know, Mr. Rosin. Just because I bought him a guitar this year doesn't mean I can't buy him a shirt next year," I said. I didn't care what he thought about any of this and I didn't care if I could change his mind. I was just keeping the conversation going as a favor to him.

"But if you only give him a shirt he will think you don't love him as much as the year you gave him the guitar."

This was the only thing I ever remembered Mr. Rosin telling me.

My job was so dull that I came home exhausted every night. Kenny couldn't understand how I could be tired from just standing around all day. I would say, "Well try doing something you don't want to do for eight hours."

And he would lecture me about how I needed to find something I wanted to do.

Kenny was like my dad in this way, always asking me what I was going to do with my life. But it seemed like the only thing I knew was what I didn't want to do. Besides, anything I had ever been enthusiastic about doing had been laughed at by my dad or teachers as unrealistic. When I was in first grade I wanted to be the world's first female brain surgeon. I used to watch *The Twenty-First Century* with Walter Cronkite on TV all the time and it had inspired me with the desire to perform the first successful brain transplant. Later on I wanted to be a marine biologist but we lived in a landlocked state. Then I wanted to be a ballerina, but I had no talent for comprehending French and moving at the same time. I was a good musician but I was only inspired to be a singer and I couldn't sing.

Even if I had been able to do these things, my dad would shoot these ideas down by laughing at me or telling me I needed to think about something where I could get insurance and a retirement plan. My mom would tell me she thought I could be anything I wanted. But she had already drilled in me for so long that where people are born is where they stay that I didn't believe her.

And maybe I was unrealistic about what I wanted, because I remember that when all the other kids went through the phase of wanting to be nuns or preachers, I only wanted to be a saint or Jesus, or at least be their girlfriend.

So I hated my job. When Kenny and his friends would talk about school stuff I felt left out, and as dull and boring as the music store. The most exciting story I had to tell people was about the stuffed dog in the bathroom of the music store. The owner had had his pet beagle stuffed when it died but his wife wouldn't let him keep it at home so he kept it at the store. Every once in a while you would hear someone scream from the bathroom when they realized it was a real dead dog and not just a stuffed toy. But by the time I'd told it for a year, that story was old. Besides, it was hard to work in when Kenny and his friends were talking about some philosophy guy or some kind of political theory.

Other than my being upset all the time, Kenny thought

I was the perfect wife. I kept a clean house, I cooked good dinners and I paid my share of the bills. And I thought Kenny was perfect too, except that I really wanted him with me more. So that day he refused to go with me to my grandparents' I started crying and told him I wasn't coming back for the whole weekend. It would be the first time since we had met over a year ago that Kenny and me hadn't slept together.

As I was leaving I said, "You're the most selfish person I've ever known. I always do what you want and I ask you for one thing and it's too much for you to give. You're no fair."

"You're a baby, Misty. Grow up and come into the world with the rest of us. Then maybe you won't feel so left out," he said as he followed me out to my car.

"You're the one who doesn't live in the real world. Why don't you just go crawl in another schoolbook. That's all you care about anyway," I cried. I hated how the more upset I would get the calmer he would become.

"Well drive safe. Try to have a good time," he said, opening my car door. "I'll see you Monday."

"Monday? So you do want me to stay away. I knew it."

"You're the one who said you wanted to stay. I don't get you. You know, sometimes I think you might be crazy."

"Oh yea! Well, fuck you, Kenny. Just fuck you." I slammed the car door shut and peeled out of the drive.

I was so angry and crying so hard I could barely see to drive. I hated Kenny, he knew I wanted him to ask me to stay. That was one of the things I hated most about guys, how they knew what you wanted from them, and they knew what you meant when you said you were leaving. Kenny knew I just wanted him to tell me he loved me and to ask me to stay. But because he didn't want to do it and he didn't want me around, he pretended like I was the one who wanted to be gone.

I felt so terrible as I pulled onto the highway, I wanted to die. Not to be dead for good, but just long enough to make Kenny see how much he wanted to be with me. I thought of the times I had run away from home, trying to get my mom and dad to realize they should treat me different, to see how sad they were without me around. Then I wondered how much I wanted to be with Kenny. I had been mad at him for so long. I felt like he was always putting me down or not paying me any attention.

I still had my crush on Jack O'Hara, which didn't seem right if I was really in love with Kenny. I remembered my dad saying once, when my mom had gone away for a while, "I don't know if I'm happier with her here and wishing she was gone or happier with her gone and wishing she was here."

Maybe too much of my parents had rubbed off on me. They didn't know the first thing about love.

All they knew was that they were miserable together and miserable apart. I couldn't figure out what I thought love was. All I knew was what I wanted it to be. I wanted love to be like it was in the beginning all the time. Loretta would tell me that was impossible because people would never get anything done if they walked around in love all the time. She had said, "You know how it is. You have to be together every minute and when you're not you're only thinking about them anyway. Even if you could stand it no one else could stand to be around you."

But I didn't want to believe that. When Kenny and me had first gotten together I felt good all the time. It was true that he skipped classes there for a while, but it was worth it. We got so much just from being near each other. From waking up and holding each other, seeing each other's face, kissing. I felt regenerated from all the horrible things in the world that had ever happened to me, just laying close to him for an hour. We would talk and listen to each other with as much excitement and passion as having sex. And we would stay up till dawn just because we couldn't get enough of each other.

But maybe I really was crazy, like Kenny said, like my dad had said. Because I honestly believed I could give up everything just to feel that way all the time. I could go on welfare and live in a trailer and not think about anything more than being with the person I loved. Kenny would tell me I was this way because I didn't know what I wanted to do with my life. And he told me that even though I might think that was the way I wanted to live I wouldn't be satisfied. He told me I was the one who had made things quit being good, because I was unhappy with who I was. Kenny said that nothing would ever have been different from the first few weeks if I had been able to realize his wanting other things didn't mean he didn't want me.

I got off the next highway exit and headed back home. I couldn't wait to get there. I felt sorry for making Kenny feel bad about having to do his work. I stopped at the grocery store to get stuff to make fried chicken, and mashed potatoes and gravy, Kenny's favorite meal. He would be happy to know I had finally come to my senses. I was never going to get mad about his working, or his friends again. I knew he loved me and I knew things really could be the same as they had been in the beginning.

WHEN I PULLED IN the driveway there was a parked car I hadn't ever seen before. I was bummed out that Kenny had company already when he'd said he had so much work to do. But I decided to stay cool and not take it as an act of treason on his part. I would even ask whoever it was if they wanted to stay for supper. When I walked up on the porch the front door was partly closed, which seemed weird because on warm days we only used the screen door. I opened the door and walked into our living room. I didn't hear anything so I figured Kenny was in the backyard or the basement.

Our house was like two lines with doors opening between each line. When you walked into the living room you followed it to the dining room, then to the kitchen, where there was a back porch. Off to the side of each room were the bedrooms and the den. Our bedroom was the first one, adjacent to the living room, then a second bedroom next to the dining room and then the den off of the kitchen. As I walked towards the back door Kenny came into the dining room from the second bedroom with his shirt open and his belt undone. He was flushed and out of breath.

"Kenny, are you OK?" I asked, worried because I thought maybe he had been crying for the whole time I was gone.

"What are you doing here?" he asked in too loud of a voice. He had a twisted smile on his face.

"Well I came back because I love you and I don't want to fight anymore. I'm sorry for getting so upset all the time," I said, setting down the groceries. I walked towards him to hold him. As I put my arms around him and turned my head to lean on his shoulder I saw a naked girl sitting on the waterbed in the second bedroom. She was sitting Indian style reading the newspaper comics. I felt like Kenny had just kicked me in the stomach. I couldn't believe I had been so stupid to think he was crying over me.

"Get her out of this house. Right now!" I said. My whole body was shaking and my hands automatically clenched into fists—I felt like I was going to explode, my heart was beating so fast. I walked into the den to wait for the girl to get out of the house.

The girl on the waterbed was a girl I hated. She was one of those girls guys said, "I don't know why you don't like her. She's a really nice person," to their girlfriends.

At parties she liked to talk to couples. She liked to talk to the guy in a couple, that is. You never caught her talking to one guy unless his girlfriend had finally got sick and walked off. She also liked to be the center of four or more guys. She would say things like "Jazz is the only music that has been created to make great love by." Guys would get in a fevered competition, loudly calling out the names of all the jazz records they owned. The first time I'd heard her say that I wished I had been able to throw up on her.

Her name was Nina Shacter and she was from the same hometown as Kenny. She was a nurse and she looked just like a nurse. She was always talking about her job, making it sound like she was smarter than any of the doctors. She'd tell stories about saving some guy's life from a doctor who'd misread a chart. Her favorite line was "Of course, if I were a doctor I wouldn't get to give massages. I love to give massages. I guess I just love to make people feel good." Nina was the kind of girl who did more damage to girls than the most asshole guy in the world could do.

I sat on the couch shaking my foot so fast the couch

was inching forward on the rug. I couldn't believe Kenny had done this to me. And done it with Nina of all people. Our house had been desecrated. At least he'd had enough loyalty not to do it in our bed.

Then I thought, Maybe he did love me, maybe he was just upset. I guessed all guys were unfaithful on some occasion. After all, we hadn't been getting along so well. Maybe he needed someone to build him up, or to take the pressure off. Then I heard Nina giggle. Nina, the girl who didn't even attempt to put her clothes on, who sat there reading the paper like this was her house. I stormed into the bedroom where she was standing, dressed and combing her hair. Kenny was standing beside the bed with the same stupid grin on his face. Nina looked over at me and said sympathetically, "I'm really sorry you had to see this. It was just one of those things, though," then she smiled all nurselike at me. What a bitch, I thought, how could she stand there and comb her hair like everything was just A-OK. Like we were some kind of happy family and I was just the pissed-off mom who would get over it in a minute. I looked at Kenny, thinking he might at least tell her to hurry up and get out or something just to defend me a little bit. But his whole face was frozen into a crazy slant.

"I hope you don't give Kenny too hard of a time." She chuckled, then said authoritatively, "That's generally how these things happen to begin with."

What could I say to that? Nothing. So I punched her as hard as I could in the face. I had never hit another person in my life except my dad, to get away from him, and my sister when we had our kid-fights.

"Get out of my house you . . . you . . . trespasser!" I yelled. She moved around me as fast as she could and ran out of the house sobbing. My car was blocking her car in the drive so she peeled through the front lawn and left deep tire tracks across my grass. Kenny's expression had finally changed and he was looking at me with horror and fear.

"You traitor! And I was going to fix you fried chicken," I cried.

Kenny didn't say anything. I guess he was afraid I had flipped and was going to kill him.

"How could you do this? I believed you when you said you had homework."

"I did. I didn't plan this. She just came over."

"Oh and so you just had to fuck her? You're that weak? I thought you were different. I thought you were committed to things and had some kind of honor. That at least you'd tell me first and not betray me," I screamed.

"I love you, Misty. You know I do."

"Well I don't love you anymore. You told me you would love me forever and be with me forever. You lied."

"You didn't ever believe that. Every day you thought I was going to leave you. There's no way to prove to someone you're going to be with them forever. All I could do was tell you and that wasn't enough for you. You made it impossible." Kenny was talking fast and waving his hands at me.

"You're going to blame me for your being a cheat and a phony and a mind fucker," I yelled back.

"You know you're crazy, Misty. I could never make you feel like I loved you. You always thought I liked someone better than I liked you and I told you you were crazy."

"Well I wasn't crazy, was I? I was right because look what you did." I thought about all the times my dad had called me crazy for believing him and my mom fought too much, or believing something was wrong with our family or saying I had lived at my grandparents'. I had known all those things were true. And now Kenny was telling me I was crazy for something that had turned out to be true. Maybe I had had a hard time thinking he loved me best but I figured if my own parents hadn't wanted me to be with them when I was born, and they had wanted Angie, there must be something wrong with me, something that made people not really want me until they didn't figure they had a choice. I was crying so hard, for so many things, I barely knew Kenny was there.

"I'm sorry this happened, Misty, more sorry than you'll ever know. But you're very hard to please. You ask for the impossible. I tell you I'll love you forever. That I always want to live together, that I want to be married someday . . . ."

"Someday? If you really knew you always wanted to be with me you'd ask me to marry you now."

"Will you marry me?" Kenny asked.

"Fuck you, Kenny. You think you're so damn smart

and I'm so stupid. You can walk out of here and tell yourself you asked me to marry you and that I said no. So you did what you could, right? But just remember you asked me after you got yourself laid by that fucking slut nurse. And all this, 'how can I prove forever' crap. I know you learned that one in your philosophy class. I read your books too. So I know that trick. So don't think you're so slick." I slammed the door as he yelled, "You're not even making sense."

I stood in the kitchen, holding on with both hands to the sink to try and keep myself from going in and slashing open the waterbed so it would flood the house.

Kenny walked in the kitchen and put his arms around me. "I'm serious, Misty, will you marry me?"

"No way, you skunk," I said, pushing his arms away from me.

"You're the one who didn't want to be together. And now you're punishing me for something you drove me to."

"You can drive an ass to water but you can't make it drink," I answered coldly.

Kenny just stood there staring at me.

When I left I drove out to Loretta's house and told her everything that happened. Loretta said, "Oh Misty. You don't know how many times I wanted to tell you about Kenny. One night when I went over to see you and you weren't home yet, Kenny tried to kiss me. We were talking on your couch and all of a sudden he reached out and tried to stick his tongue in my mouth. I jumped up and ran out of the house. I didn't know what to do. I was so confused, but he was drunk and high so I tried to just lay it off to that."

"He tried to have sex with you?"

"Well I believe he would've, he didn't have a chance to get that far," Loretta said.

I couldn't believe Kenny had done what Loretta had said. I could but I couldn't. I remembered all the times I had told her how much I trusted him and I felt like a fool.

I stayed at Loretta's that night and moved back to my parents' the next day. It was hard packing all the things me and Kenny had gotten together. I cried when I wrapped up the crystal paperweights and dishes and silverware we had bought at auctions. And we even almost fought over the blood-red goblets as I wrapped them in tissue paper. Kenny said they were his. But I just stared at him and said, "Do you need them to entertain with?"

The only other thing Kenny said to me that day was as I was leaving. "I'll call you, Misty," he called out as I walked to my car.

I had never even told my mom and dad that Kenny and me lived together but it was unspoken knowledge that we did. My dad bitched at first, saying I was going to be sponging off him the rest of my life, but basically they were happy to have me home again.

Angie had just moved back home again too. She had gotten divorced from a guy she had married her senior year of high school. It was a stupid marriage—Angie had gotten pregnant and refused to get an abortion. The guy she married was a loser, he beat her and couldn't hold a job. But I guess getting married had been part of Angie's rebellion.

Angie had a son now and it was nice, all of us living together. It was so nice that I was almost forgetting what we had been like before, and thought maybe we did have a family like the ones on TV.

When I told Angie what had happened with me and Kenny she told me he had tried to come on to her a few times too. Once even when she was holding the baby.

Every girlfriend I had told me, after I broke up with Kenny, "I wanted to tell you but I didn't know how. You trusted him so much. But he tried the same thing with me."

After Kenny I had a hard time trusting guys. At first I thought Kenny was the first guy who had betrayed me but after a while I realized all the guys I had known had betrayed me in one way or another. Darryl had betrayed me the day he ran out on me when my dad had found us naked. Darcy, Pam's husband, had betrayed me and her by trying to get me to sleep with him. Actually they had both asked me to sleep with them right after they got married. I did, but I was only sixteen and I only did it because Pam begged me to. After that happened, though, I guess Darcy thought I was loose because he kept trying to get me to have sex with him behind Pam's back. I tried to be nice at first and just say no but I finally had to start being mean so he'd leave me alone. Then

Pam quit being friends with me because she said I was rude to her husband. The only thing I learned from that experience was that I would never go to bed with more than one person again, even for my best friend.

Stuart Kyle had betrayed me by not telling me we were breaking up. One of my dad's best friends, who had known me since I was a baby, and I thought was my friend too, had tried to French-kiss me and would have done more if I hadn't stopped him in horror. Mickey Beechum had betrayed me by never talking to me again after I had let him feel me up in church. Russ Baker had broken his word when he promised to come back to me. And of course there was my dad.

I thought about the first summer I had lived with my mom and dad. One night my dad had to come to the hospital to pick me up. Me and my mom and Angie had been in a car wreck. They were pretty badly hurt and had to stay in the hospital. While the nurses waited for my dad to come for me they put me down in a metal, crib-like bed. It was the only thing I remembered about the car wreck—laying in the bed and looking up at my dad. He was leaning over the silver bars and rubbing my hand between his hands. A young nurse was standing next to him and smiling softly at us. My dad had tears in his eyes and was trying to smile. As he touched my cheek he said, "Everything is going to be OK. You're safe, I'm here now. I'll make sure you're never hurt or scared or sad again, Misty. I'll always keep you safe."

So maybe I'd had a problem with trust for a long time.

Kenny had always told me that as hard as he tried he could never make me believe him. I wanted to believe him, though. I wanted to feel trust as much as I wanted to float on my back in a crystal-blue river. To hear the waves lap gently against the shore, feel the sun shining down on my face. I wanted to close my eyes and feel warm and weightless, to drift with the motion of the water. That's what I wanted. But the reality was that my eyes wouldn't be closed—they'd be clenched shut and my body would be rigid, not weightless. And I would try to concentrate on the feeling of warmth from the sun and the peaceful sounds of the water lapping against the rocks. But underneath it all my brain would be frenzied with thoughts of copperheads, leeches, whirlpools and sex-starved rednecks, drunk and lurking on the riverbanks. And maybe I had felt this way a lot longer than I had known.

EVEN THOUGH EVERYONE seemed to think I was aimless and didn't know what I wanted in my life I knew for certain that I would never marry someone in Springfield or that I would live in Springfield the rest of my life.

Kenny tried to get me to come back to him for months after I broke up. Darryl had done the same thing—told me he loved me and wanted to get married. Darryl did that after he had broken up with me and I had started going out with Gene Sylvester. I wouldn't have married Kenny or Darryl, even if they had asked me when we first fell in love. I don't think so, anyway.

Actually, for Jack O'Hara, I believed that I would forsake my commitment to leave Springfield. But after what had happened with Kenny I felt especially awful that I slept with Jack. I'd get to feeling guilty and remember that Loretta had rejected Kenny. Then I'd try to make myself feel better and I'd think, she wasn't really attracted to Kenny to begin with. It's not that hard to be true to your convictions when the temptation is not so great.

Jack and me left Kenny's party that night after he had flirted with me the whole time there. I knew we were going to be together when he had walked over and asked, "Do you want to play Columbus?"

"What's that?" I responded without meeting his eyes.

"Well you're America and I'm Columbus and I get to discover you." Then he handed me a beer and said, "I've always wanted to live in your country." It was pouring rain and as I was leaving Jack came up to me and said, "Let's carpool."

"OK," I said. I was feeling as shy and excited as if he had already kissed me.

We drove back to his house and stayed up and drank beer and talked about him and Loretta, me and Kenny, me and Gene, me and Darryl, me and Stuart. Jack told me he knew that me and Gene would never last, then he said, "That guy was a human death warrant. How could you have ever been with him to begin with?"

"I don't know. I wonder why I've done a lot of things," I said.

Then Jack started kissing me and while he was kissing me he whispered, "I've wanted to be with you since the first time I ever saw you."

I melted and fell even more deeply in love.

"I've always been crazy over you."

"Well, I've always been crazy," I said. I felt confused because I didn't know what it meant for Jack to be with Loretta when he said he had wanted to be with me. Then I thought about Kenny trying to be with other girls the whole time we were together, but begging me to come back to him after he knew I was gone. It didn't make sense to think that the only way you were really desired by a guy was when you weren't with them. It seemed like as soon as they got you under their power, with silky lines and promises and sexy ways, they left you. Not literally, because conquered territory was still important to hold, but it wasn't as exciting as something new and foreign.

I laid in bed next to Jack, who whispered for a long time after we were through about how great he felt. I knew he would go back to Loretta the next day and we would be a memory unless I let him do it again. I knew he loved Loretta and I knew that even if he did break up with her there would never be a chance for us. Because

I would always know that he loved Loretta most, even if he didn't know it. I believed that anyone I would ever be with would always love the person they were with before me best. And if I did happen to find a virgin, I knew I would believe he could only love someone he hadn't been with more than he could love me.

I didn't know if this was a deeply romantic notion I held or if I had finally and fully turned into my mom.

My mom was the only person who didn't hate Kenny for what he had done to me. When I told her what had happened she said, "You didn't really want to be with Kenny or you'd be with him. You only want a fella who's going to give you a hard time and if he won't do it on his own you'll force him to."

"What do you mean?" I asked, wondering why she didn't feel bad for me.

"I mean, it's clear by the boys you pick. You don't pick nice ones and when you do you're mean to them."

My mom was drunk, I could tell now. She had that challenger look. It was the phase she passed through just before self-pity, which was just before passing out.

Maybe I had always known my mom was an alcoholic. But I remembered the day I first called her one. I was a junior in high school and a lady from AA had come to speak in my sociology class. When she described how she had hidden her liquor in places like laundry detergent bottles and perfume bottles and vinegar bottles I knew she was also talking about my mom. The lady said that alcoholism was a physical disease and that a person shouldn't feel shame because they couldn't drink. Then she talked about how low she had to get before she went for help. Even she hadn't gone and drank in the tunnels under the railroad tracks like my mom had. She hadn't fallen and given herself a concussion and she hadn't tried to kill herself.

I came home that night and told my mom about the lady from AA. I said, "Mom, why don't you try going to AA. I think you're an alcoholic. It's nothing to be ashamed of. She said it isn't."

"All alcoholics say that. That's how I know I'm not one. Why is it this is the only kind of junk you listen to in school? I've learned one thing about you by now, Misty. If there's fifty people talking in a room and only one of them is a wacko, you're the one who'll be listening, ears up, to the wacko. Well don't try to pin me up in any of your menageries."

I cried the rest of that night. When my dad came in later I was mean to him. I really blamed him for my mom's condition because every time he'd go away for a few days my mom would get drunk. She didn't know how else to not hurt so bad.

Still, I didn't like to talk to my mom when she was drinking because she always tried to start a fight with me. I'd usually try to avoid it but sometimes she'd say such nasty things I'd have to defend myself.

"I was never mean to Kenny," I said, wanting to keep my mouth shut but not being able to. It was hard to let her get away with saying certain things to me.

"You treated him like a puppy dog. You're just like your Aunt Louise," she sneered as she lit a cigarette.

"I did not and I am not. Why don't you go lay down, Mom?" I could feel myself go to the same place I always went to in these moments. It was a combination of wanting to lay down and sleep and feeling anxious and violent.

"Kenny did whatever you wanted him to do. You used him. It served you right for him to do what he did to you." She grinned.

"Why are you always against me?" I asked, feeling tears in my eyes.

"No one's ever against the high and mighty Misty Groves," my mom slurred, "the bold and beautiful bitch."

"You don't know what you're talking about. He betrayed me."

My mom's idea of who I was had gotten more distorted over the years. She believed that because I had freed myself from her, I was out there conquering and winning the world. I guess if I hadn't left Kenny she would be able to care about what he had done to me. But since she hadn't left my dad for all he'd done to her it only made her hate me. She had decided I did it because I was so strong but I thought I did it because I couldn't stand the pain it had caused me.

"He asked you to marry him."

"So what?"

"So, he was a good man. But you just want to ruin your life. To be a whore."

I knew my mom had liked Kenny a lot because he was nice to her and would talk to her. She thought he was going to be rich and successful and I guess she figured I had blown my chance for that.

Most of the time I didn't think my mom meant all the things she said to me when she was drunk but other times I thought when she was drunk was the only time she did mean the things she said. So often she had told me she hated me and that I was a failure that I thought it didn't hurt me anymore. But thinking she believed Kenny was a better person than me, that I deserved to be deceived by him, made me feel really bad.

Since I had moved back home and things seemed better I guess it came as a bigger shock each time bad things happened. It seemed like since my mom and dad had quit fighting so much she had started trying to fight with me more. My mom was never so mad at Angie because Angie had a kid. My mom believed Angie would now have to suffer as much burden in her life she had. Even though she said she wanted our lives to be better than hers, she really didn't, she wanted them to be just as horrible as she felt hers had been so we could say, "I know why you do the things you do."

It was hard for me to know how my mom felt about

me. She was either telling me she would never be able
to live without me or telling me I had, and always would,
ruin her life.

I hated my mom but I loved her. And besides, maybe
she was right about me. Maybe no matter how old I got
I always would be jailbait. Because maybe I would only
ever be able to love the kind of guys who could've been
locked up behind dark mesh in the Stone County
courthouse.

When I had been with Gene Sylvester was the only time
I had loved a guy with no intention of it lasting forever.
The first time I saw him was at a bar where he was a
drummer in a rock 'n' roll band. He was a really great
musician but that wasn't what got my attention. At the
end of the night, after the last set the band played, Gene
broke open a beer bottle against his drums and slashed
his face with it. The next weekend when I saw the
band again, he walked over to me and said, "You gotta
car?"

I nodded and he said, "I'm really beat. Will you take
me home?"

The palms of my hands were wet as I slid them against
the inside of my coat pockets to search for my keys.

Gene was grisly-looking. His face was scarred and
whiskery. He had a prison-type haircut while all the other
guys in town had long hair. Gene didn't talk much but
when he did his voice was dry and gravelly. He looked
to be about forty, even though at the time forty was an

unimaginable age to me for anyone to be except parents.

People were shocked that I liked Gene. But there was something about him that excited me and scared me and made me feel strong at the same time. Maybe it was because I knew no matter how I tried I'd never be as crazy as he was.

That night I left the bar with Gene I invited him over to my house. I knew we would end up sleeping together but I figured he would at least talk to me first. We sat on my couch for a few minutes and he didn't say a word. I got up to go to the bathroom, feeling nervous as he watched me cross the room. When I came out all the lights were off. I thought Gene had left, but when I walked in my bedroom he was standing there naked. He walked over and undressed me.

Sex with Gene was like walking into oblivion. I didn't know what I liked best—the way my body was filled with total sensation or the way my brain came to a dead stop. With Gene you didn't need to have responsibility or conscience or hope.

Gene was a desperate guy, deeply and sincerely tortured. You could tell by the way he rode his motorcycle. There was absolutely no future in Gene's eyes. And even though I didn't think I believed in that sort of stuff anymore Gene did have a really short lifeline.

One night we were watching TV and a drummer was on some interview show. While he was playing the drums Gene started to cry. I got real nervous. I hadn't ever seen a guy cry that way before.

"He is a true artist. So pure. I'll never be free till I can reach that stretch," he said with tears.

"Oh," I answered. I didn't understand at all what he was saying. I wanted Gene to leave but I was always kind of afraid of him and I was thinking if I asked him to leave when he was crying he might get mad and break something. We didn't talk for about an hour and then I told him I had to get up early and that he had to go.

Gene was the sexiest guy I had known but I guess I always thought it meant there was something bad wrong with me that I like a guy who slashed his face open.

I never really wanted to quit being with Gene but I made myself keep my distance from him. It took a long time for me to get Gene out of my system.

I'VE TRIED TO FIND the one thing that connects all my boyfriends so I could decide if I have a particular type or if I'm just repeating a bad pattern. If I had never been with Mark Roth I would never have tried to figure this out.

I met Mark when Woody Allen was still a big deal, which was the reason I fell for him. Mark Roth was exotic by Missouri standards—he was funny, he was Jewish, he was from New York City and he had been to lots of shrinks. Mark always said he believed everyone needed a shrink.

We went together about a year and in that year Mark tried to make me aware of how messed up I was because of my family. We'd get in a lot of fights where I'd want him to give me some evidence that he was improved by all his hours on the couch. He didn't seem more normal than me. He had sex problems, I didn't have sex problems, I'd had lots of sex. But Mark would tell me that was proof I needed help, and that if I didn't get it I'd be doomed to live my parents' lives for the rest of mine.

When my mom found out I had started going to a shrink she went berserk. First she cried for an hour on her bed. Every once in a while I'd poke my head in her room to say, "It's really not that big a deal, Mom." Finally I figured if I let her alone she would get over it quicker, so I settled down to eat the brownies she had made and wait for her to recover. When I heard her door slam I could tell which side of the door she was on. I braced myself, waiting for her to come into the kitchen. She stomped up to the table and yanked a chair from under the table. Her eyes were red and she was puffing a cigarette and blowing the smoke out onto my brownies.

"I suppose they tell you everything is all my fault, that I'm a terrible mother and that I made you crazy."

"I'm not crazy, Mom. I believe everybody should go to a psychiatrist." My voice almost had a New York accent and I was talking in the same withdrawn way that Mark had talked to me when I got upset.

"Well I don't need one to know nothing would ever be good enough for you. You can tell your fancy head doctor that he can talk to you till he's blue and you won't listen to him either."

"It's not a he. And she doesn't try to make me think a certain way. She listens," I said nonchalantly, knowing that if what I was saying wasn't enough to make her mad the way I was saying it was.

My mom's body was shaking and so stiff it looked like she was shaking against it. She stood that way a few seconds, then grabbed the plate of brownies and threw them into my lap. "Do you tell this Ms. Doctor of yours about all the goddamn treats I fix for you? About all the clothes I didn't buy so you could dress like a princess? All the meals I ate at home so you could have your McDonald's snacks whenever you wanted?"

"Material things aren't so important as you think. Anyone can give that."

"Oh anyone can? Well, honey, you just find anyone to give you that and good luck," she screamed. "I bet your lady doctor doesn't have any kids of her own. She was too smart for that. She'll just make money off all the poor slobs who did.

"I love the way all these know-it-all assholes can sit on their high horse and talk about what a bad parent is. What a bad mother is. They just love to stick it to the mother and dear old Dad gets off scot-free.

"But for all their bullshit I'll tell you that when they do have kids—which is rare—they have the most abnormal ones of the lot. I teach their kids, the ones they didn't have time to raise because they're too busy telling everyone else how to raise theirs.

"And their poor kids, they're always the troublemakers. They all end up in jail, on drugs or in psychiatric wards. Look at Melissa Shumacher. With all his money and fancy psychiatrist voodoo, her father couldn't fix her. Could he? Even your regular doctors can't raise a healthy kid. Their kids are all riddled with some disease or other.

"These people with their better-than-thou attitudes are going to try and tell me I don't know how to raise a kid. Why hell, I not only raised my own I raise theirs five days a week."

I was completely out of breath when my mom finished her speech. But I was more relaxed because I knew it always calmed her down to be able to go on like that without someone calling her crazy or hitting her.

My dad's reaction when I told him I was seeing a psychiatrist was a little different. I told him as he was trimming the hedges in our backyard. He just said, "Well I guess you need one because anyone who would waste money on that kind of crapola is a definite crazy." Then he told me to go make him a glass of iced tea.

Shrinks had no power over my dad because it wouldn't matter what they said, he wouldn't buy it. But my mom was a believer. The truth was she would've liked to talk to someone that way—about her problems, about life— but she knew my dad would never let her go, so she just got mad and bitter at me for being able to. Of course, really the only reason I even started going to a shrink was because a boyfriend had told me to, which can't be that different from my mom not going because my dad told her not to.

It's hard to remember why or how me and Mark broke up because it took so long—half of the time we were together. Me and Mark probably never should've been together, we were really only friends and I never had a very deep romance for him.

When I broke up with Mark I told Dr. Madigan I had made a pact with myself to never again get involved with a guy until I knew for sure he was the one I wanted to spend the rest of my life with. If it meant that I would be alone the rest of my life I was prepared to be alone. I could still fool around but I would never again fall in love until I met the guy who could meet every one of my requirements.

I believed that so far I had only gotten little parts of what I wanted in each guy. Now I wouldn't be satisfied or content until I had someone who was everything in one.

I wanted someone who kissed the way Gene Sylvester kissed—with the excitement and newness of the very first time we touched and the desperation and longing of the last time it would ever be.

I wanted someone like Kenny Rochester—a person who wasn't just shaped by his experience but who shaped his experiences. Someone with ideas and convictions.

I wanted someone like Mark Roth, who sort of liked to think about psychology stuff. Someone like Darryl Clement, who was a little lazy. Someone like Jack O'Hara, who was cool and sexy. Someone like Stuart Kyle, who was sort of into being responsible—though he hadn't been too responsible to me. Of course, he probably was so responsible that he had a really boring job. I didn't want anyone that responsible, but just kind of responsible in the way that if you were crossing the street together he would look out for the traffic and put his arm out to guard you if you weren't paying attention.

And I wanted someone like Russ Baker, who believed we would always be together. Sometimes I wished I could have married Russ—that we had stayed together since we were kids. We wouldn't be like those couples who meet each other in their twenties or thirties, having to tell each other about our pasts, we would have lived it all together. We wouldn't have to imagine who the other one had been with, what each other's life had been like before we met or what each other had looked like. And we would always be young kids together because that was what we were when we met.

I quit seeing Dr. Madigan soon after me and Mark broke up. I don't know how much I actually got out of going to her. She did tell me I focused on boys too much, when what I really should be looking at was the relationship I had with my parents. She made it clear that she thought my mom was the root of my problems. And that my dad was the victim of her insanity. I guess I believed her for a while, but it always felt like a betrayal, not just to my mom but to everyone who ended up being blamed for things that really weren't their fault.

I believed guys wanted to be responsible for you. It was when you finally gave in and let them that they couldn't handle it—they got pissed off at you, they cheated on you, they called you weak or they hit you.

My mom wasn't responsible for my dad leaving her alone all the time, Loretta's mom wasn't responsible for Mr. Lindsy having affairs on her. Angie wasn't responsible for her husband beating her. I wasn't responsible for that Primrose creep doing what he wanted with me. And Laura Campbell's mom probably wasn't even responsible for being insane. Because if Mr. Campbell hadn't let Laura's mom guilt-trip him the way she did everyone else, if he had left her early on, before she'd had so many kids they couldn't take care of, if he had done that then maybe she'd at least still have half a mind.

As far as I could see it most women hadn't become victims because of their weakness, they had been made victims because they were physically weaker.

The last thing Dr. Madigan said to me was "There are avoiders and there are confronters. There are those who blame others for their problems and become victims and those who try to examine their own weaknesses. Perhaps someday you'll have the courage and initiative to fix your own life. Perhaps you will try to be different from your mother and not look for a male figure to be responsible for you or your mistakes."

What she said sounded smart and strong and independent. But then I realized this was just the kind of thing Nina Shacter, the nurse, would say. Nina Shacter would have said that to a girl in front of her boyfriend, she would have said that to a group of guys to describe other women. Then I knew that Dr. Madigan was full of shit.

Even though I didn't trust Dr. Madigan on most things, I knew I didn't want to end up like my mom or my dad or half the other people who lived in Springfield. I was twenty-five and I still didn't know what I wanted to do. But I knew I had to go away for good from this place.

Mark Roth was moving back to New York so I decided to move there too, since that was the only place other than Springfield, Thelma and Galena where I knew anyone. I gave myself six months to save money and emotionally prepare for my final farewell to home.

Breaking up with Springfield wasn't that different from breaking up with any of the guys I had left. I spent the first three months remembering all the things that had kept me there—my friends, the familiarity, how much my family needed me. I spent the last three months thinking of the reasons I needed to leave—the familiarity, my parents' fights and the fact there was nothing I could do that would ever save them from who they were.

Maybe because I was so old by the time I had decided to go out on my own I became obsessed with the idea I had wasted so much time in my life. I would watch the second hand go around the face of a clock and remember how I used to sit in the rocking chair in my parents' living room. How I would watch the clock and pray to see them drive down our hill before the second hand had made a full circle. It would seem like it would take forever. Now, in a breath, a whole second of my life was lessened. I would try not to breathe so much. I would try not to look at the time, or know dates, or pay my bills, because then I'd have to know another month had slipped away to where. Time gone by had become the same as death to me. I didn't know where it went to. If it went somewhere else to be saved, to be lived again or visited. What had happened to all the times I had been in love and believed it would last the rest of my life? What happened to all the days I had lived with my mom and my dad and Angie? If they had died someone would say to me, "But no one can take your memories away."

But a memory didn't seem like enough to hold on to —and pretty soon that was all my mom and dad, my home would be to me. A memory was only like a TV show, it could make you laugh or cry or happy while you saw it but you couldn't really touch it, no matter how keen your senses were or how vivid your imagination. A memory was not a thing you could grab hold of and be grabbed back by. It wasn't something shared and physical. A memory was only exactly what it was.

My Aunt Eve had become a memory before I was even born. All the guys I had thought I loved were a memory.

My mom's tenderness and hope had become a memory. Angie's innocence was a memory. And all the ideas I had about people before I really knew them were memories.

I wondered why if love could go away, if that meant the love isn't real. I wondered if who my mom and dad were now was who they really were, or were they the people they had been before pain and loss and hardship had changed them. And would they ever be those people again, the ones I could see sometimes when things were good and life felt easy to them.

I thought about the day me and my dad had gone to the river and found the owl that had been struck by the bolt of lightning, how it was clinging to the log because it wanted so much to stay somewhere familiar. My dad had told me that was a death grip. Maybe that was what being able to remember was. Just like my dad had walked off with the owl's claw and I had given it away to get something back, so had everyone I'd touched walked away with a part of me that they would pass off to someone else, hoping to get something back. I guess if me and my dad hadn't come along and taken the claw from that owl he might not even be a memory. He would just have washed off down the river eventually and no one would even know he had been there. The owl stayed alive because my dad had made a trophy of his claw. He became bigger and more awesome and grand because we had taken his claw and given him life in places he would never have otherwise lived.